Wendy Waite
Collected Works

Edited by Jonathan Murray

OTTER PRESS

Charlotte, North Carolina

Cover art: Original lithograph by Jayne Johnson
Book design by Mervil M. Paylor
Author photograph by Jonathan Murray

ISBN 0-9786527-0-3

Published by Otter Press, Inc., Charlotte, North Carolina

The idea for creating *Collected Works* arose shortly after Wendy's death on June 28, 2005, from ovarian cancer. Having had the unalloyed joy of being Wendy's husband and sharing Wendy's life for 16 years, I was witness to much of Wendy's effort in creative writing. However, it wasn't until I started going through her personal papers that I fully realized the extent of what those efforts had brought to fruition on the page.

Much of Wendy's creative writing reflects a childlike fascination for the natural world and the creatures that inhabit that world. Indeed, when she wasn't busy with work or other more mundane responsibilities, she wanted little else but to *be* in that world. I couldn't count the hours I watched Wendy scouring a 20-foot stretch of mountain stream or a 200-yard stretch of ocean beach completely immersed in the sights, the scents, the sounds, the *now* of the natural world. In many of her works, most especially in her poems, Wendy found a resonance between this outer natural world and her own inner creative world. In publishing *Collected Works*, it is my hope that others may be able to glimpse, through Wendy's own words, her unique vision of both worlds.

Collected Works is organized into 5 chapters. The individual works within each of the first four chapters are all arranged in rough chronological order. Most of the works were written between 1989 and 2005. The first chapter, "How to Build a Hummingbird," is a collection of twenty-nine of Wendy's most poignant poems incorporated as a kind of chapbook within *Collected Works*. "Sounding" was originally published in *The Beloit Poetry Journal* in the winter 1993/1994 edition. The version of "River Otters Return to Briar Creek" in "Essays and Stories" is slightly longer than the version that originally appeared in *The*

Charlotte Observer on September 7, 2004, where economy of words was an issue, and it is reprinted with the permission of *The Charlotte Observer*; copyright owned by *The Charlotte Observer*. "Squirrels on the Seesaw" was originally produced as a radio essay and was broadcast on WFAE public radio in Charlotte on June 3, 2005. At the time of her death, Wendy was working on "Abelarde and Heloise" in "Works for Children"as an illustrated book. The other two works in this chapter are written in a style of verse that suggests Wendy's intention of publishing them in the form of illustrated books as well.

While not a creative work in the same sense as the other works in this book, I thought it important that "The Second Sex, the Third World, and the Fourth Estate" was included. As an Assistant Professor of Communications at Queens University of Charlotte, Wendy delivered this speech on March 17, 2004, as a part of the Women's History Month lecture series at Queens University. The speech was subsequently published in *Vital Speeches of the Day*, April 15, 2004. In this speech, one can get a real sense of Wendy's dedication to journalism and the women who have become an irreplaceable part of it.

The completion of *Collected Works* would not have been possible without the help of many of Wendy's colleagues and friends. In particular, I would like to thank the following: Julie Funderburk, Craig Renfroe, Charles Israel, and Tammy Woody for their assistance in the editing process; Anthony Abbot for helping with poem selection in "How to Build a Hummingbird"; Jayne Johnson for creating the cover art; Mervil Paylor and Jane Siemens for helping with book design and manuscript preparation.

— Jonathan Murray, *Editor*

Contents

Other Poems

How to Build a Hummingbird

How to Build a Hummingbird

Your thumb would make two of him
but you mustn't use that. No shortcuts
allowed. All it takes is all you are

and more than that. With your art
use hope and muster, take the air
behind his wings and the space

where the bird may be, and the part
of you that breaks with the blur
of him. With wings do the best you can.

When you begin he has no more
scent than stones in deep water.
With your breath give him ocean

spray, cedar and scent of cotton
and though you are finished
with him you know he is not done

with you when he lifts at last from
the heresy of your hand, your first
day, the beginning of everything

HEAT STRESS

1

The fires have been climbing the mountains for weeks
before we start dreaming fire
scorch, firebreath, summer curtains billowing flame
like furies over our bed, muses of hell
and   waking   see smoke
from a dozen new ones fogging
Forty Acre Rock.
By the time we split up the fires have seared
everything green.
                    All the fires
ashes and crisped grass.

2

No rain for months, and the county agent
says the chickens are in trouble
"Well, he'll start in to stretching his neck out
and pretty soon after that he'll be dead
and once he does that
theren't very much you can do fer'im."
A thousand dead birds, then thousands
by autumn   but it always comes back around:
fierce cerulean sky
                    fire in the trees.

3

The lake is pocked with turtle heads
and in the shallows the Canada geese are out of control
wings like windmills pump this one under; he otters
through the redbrown murk like some foreign animal
the others circle and stretch
their necks out, hiss at each other
churn the water to silver

then they stop.
The lake heaves, smooths with relief.

4

Brittle days, fires to the north
smoke the sky three hundred miles away.
Yesterday the ginkgoes down the road
blazed with yellow bright enough to read by
this morning all that yellow blankets the ground
obeying as always that flex in the air or light
     it's time it's time it's time

we wait in our smoky room
for the lakes to hear an echoing flex
climb down from the mountains again
quench our fiery dreams.

COUNTERBALANCE

I put seed out once again this morning
and once again by evening it's entirely
gone, eaten up, the feeders swing quite empty.
And bobbing on the branches, the little monsters
waiting for more, and quick and flick and waiting.
Of course I put out more, and drink my coffee,
and try to reconstruct my lost ambition.

A windowledge bird, gleam and gray and flutter
so close, his brilliant eye, his sweet wild breathing
and feathers lift and blow; the air is icy
the window foggy from the radiator.
He takes a seed and turns and preens and cracks it.
He must not sense me. All the glass reflects
is bird, himself, crape myrtles behind him.

Now dry hulls drift and drop, coffee cools
while feathers on a bird's throat crack my heart.

CYCLES

I heard the barred owl last night for the first
time in weeks. Between now and mid-May
she and her mate will nest and raise two fledglings.
She has lived here for years, right in the city's
wooded park, so close to the skyscrapers.
Each year I seek the nest, and so this morning
after you left, I struck out to find her.
Of course it was no use: why does she always
choose a different tree?

     Last time I heard her
was the night I met you, and her calling
cooled and soothed my terror.

     So now it starts
again, the brilliant pain, hinges thick
with rust, dust, open slowly, or don't open.
It's too soon. It's not soon enough. Each way
is truth. And either way, I'm unprepared
and clumsy, and have nothing much to say.

When I reach the water that cuts skylit
through the park, I stop to watch a grackle
preen, splash and drink, and then take flight
oilslick rainbow colors in his blackness
there, though hard to see, as wings hit shadow.

My mother
my mother with high blood pressure
my mother is dressing a baked potato.
She loves them dripping butter
but ever since her father died
heart attack at fifty
her potatoes have been austere works
dry, modestly cleft
merest pat of Country Morning Blend
herb seasoning, salt-free, of course.
This potato
this potato she is fixing
is different, slit to the foil
salt-crusted, gorged with sour cream
and as I watch she hacks a slab of butter
smears the mess together, wailing.
I missed the fight this time
it was over before I came home from play
        practice
my father gone off to wherever he goes.
I edged past to practice my lines.
Looking back from a quarter-century
all I see
are my mother's cheek on the white formica
my mother's open-frozen mouth
my mother's potato
heaped mounds of butter dripping
over its seared and crisped skin.

In the Dream, it's Always April

and she comes, arriving by bus
and there she is *it's your arm?*

her arm in a cast *it's just*
your arm? it's April and warm

apple scent comes with her
we were sure you were dead

but she is here, and it's her
arm, no more than a broken

arm, and I cry, and she cries
but the tire — all of us thought

you were dead — that blown tire
but in the dream, that was all

a mistake, some other dream
when they called across three

state lines, the telephone's urgent
buzz, a dream, some other apple-

fragrant April when the very air
was full of astonished flowers

for Cindy

The dream of hearth and woman would begin
after Korea. He **pulled through** and **came
home to her.** That's how they talked back then
in their L-frame fescued house (she took his name

the way they did), pot roast, her mother. Ten
years. Twenty. He left her and us three
kids to write and find himself again,
go west, something. She drank, watched TV

in pink foam curlers, pulled the whole thing in
around her, sitcoms, soaps, **patience of Job**
she said, **patience of Job. But girl that man
would drive old Job to drink,** that terry robe.

When it frayed she held it together with a pin.

From animals you learned Animal.
Before the consonants for *mama*
you sang Animal in your crib, practicing
at daybreak *braak skree aow rrra* each call
learned from crickets and neighborhood toms.
Soon enough you learned *cat* and, naming it,
learned the cat says *meow*, and never sang
Animal again.
                Years later I heard you cry
beyond words, swallowing playground taunts
though your mother sang that useless
ditty about sticks and stones, a chant

I could not recall when the man who vowed
to protect and cherish curled his tongue
around the syllables of my name and spat
them at me, as if their shape and pitch
scorched the soft tissues of his throat.

I didn't remember Animal until long after
he left, my howl and cry beginning at last
to revolve into words, names that build walls
between the thing and the one who thinks.

The sound of *distance* singing, a song
like breath sliding in and out of its sheath
like blood burning back into frozen hands
like Eve after Eden, unnaming everything.

Here it is March, and I've had to scrape
ice, frost really, from my windshield
just once. Daffodils in February
and not even a hard freeze to slick
them with ice in the mornings.

"Greenhouse," they say, explaining it.
Greenhouse, lifesource, warm wet
spongy loam, air full of roots
and rain, breathe it or drink it.
They don't mean it that way.

I always imagined taking my daughter
across the field, ice crystaled
on weedstalks, in dirt, to the pond
show her how, two feet of ice above
the fish still move.

Winter warmed. The dream changed.
Tell her how it used to be:
winters so cold
the very rain would freeze
of something like that, but now

it doesn't matter. She waited
too long to come. Winter changed
years before I gave up my own cycles
along with the dream of cupping her name
from the heart of fire, like ice.

like the *hallelujah* of a laughing gull
or the spray light makes on rough water
or a spider web, like the crash and pull
of waves on the walls of the Battery.

Chee-Yun plays Spoleto, and the main
truth I want you to know is when her
bow slips from the strings of the violin
and she plays the strands of her hair

the music knows no difference, nor
do you. The music rises, turns
sound now to light, now to color
like the scarf of the Gullah weaver

in the market, or the ancient nautilus
you find in the gem shop fossilized,
become opal, jasper, agate, crystal
hold time, just this minute, just this

and as you hold it the minerals begin
to dissolve, the sunshot opal first, then
each grain, each crystal replaced by skin
by shell and muscle, eye and brain

running backward the reel of the earth
until sheer stone returns to the surge
and pulse of the living animal, here
in your hand, astonished at the world

grown a million years, ten million older
but it knows the music and its race
and the sea, and the way back there.
Let it go. You have no choice.

She's on the spire again. She shifts
in the sunlight, here on the cross at the top
of the Baptist Church, where her one surviving
fledgling launched last April. She called
for hours before at last he took
the uncertain air to his breast and rose
on a thermal easy as breathing, his cries
playing me, bone and sense, like ancient
fire. Like grace.

When Itszak Perlman
bowed that great unplayable concerto,
our screams and pounding applause at the end
swelled beyond our will. We urged
him back and back, helpless to stop
clapping, to pull our adulation
away as he battled his withered legs
across the stage again and again
and again to our love.

The hawk on the cross
on the spire of the church flares her redfire
tail as the paean starts and the carillon
sings in her blood. The spire alive
with sound, the bird shifts with the bass,
screams and shrugs her wings, then leaps
lifted with wind, with heat and song
as close to heaven as we can hurl
anything.

MIGRATION

After my lover left me yet again
heading for Florida and ten days
without me, after I untwined my limbs
from his and let him go, I turned
to the hummingbird we had scooped
from near the grave three weeks before
to revive with prayer and nectar.

I called it cage behavior at first
the pattern he followed this fall,
a droning incessance no purpose
seemed to justify:
first his turned
head, then a lifted
wing, dip and fall
into a tight
buzzing circle
back to the same
forked branch
again and again
and again. But his blood
was singing beyond the cage
fly now   fly now   fly now

For his own great good I kept him close.
Held back from that wild imperative,
wired urgency of his kind, he fell,
south wind on his wings, into all
that was left that he could do.

The way my grandmother, before she died
kept throwing herself from the bed.
Or how my lover, his circle complete
for this year at least, returned one more time
to his own branched tree.

The radio host with the broken voice
is talking with a Chinese girl too plain
for men, who bound her own lotus feet
beginning when she was seven. The pain
was worse at night. Her toes cracked, filled
with pus, drained. She left the bindings on.

In Charleston during festival season we wear
slides or sandals, go barefoot, feel the tide turn.

Just above the Battery an espalier flaunts
a single huge flower like a Christmas tree
star, so heavy with fragrance it pulls
away from the brick facade, spilling scent
like heat and cut lemons. First time I've seen
them do that to a magnolia, that Southern

giant, backyard sentinel, guardian
of Mississippi childhood. We pinned leaves
big as angel wings to our shirts and climbed
branches so low and full we needed no boost,
played all day in leaves enough to tent. Now
the shape is in the heads of the landscape

architects, who can't say when hot stone will burn
the stunned foliage. Where it might bloom.

How to Enter a Mountain Creek

Slowly, the way you pulled on your first
pair of nude stockings before the dance;
slowly, for the way the stream's edge
makes you gasp; slowly, letting your numbed

feet start to adjust as the chill and pulse
of the creek rises to your knees, your thighs,
between your legs and up where the scar
begins; now slide down and down and allow

the water to follow the scar up your belly
to your breast, your throat, and at last
your scalp. Nothing like the mud turtle
you found stranded, waiting for hours

or days, stunned by the heat
and the shock of the wall of webbing
left by crews cutting a road beside
the stream; how, when you lifted him over

the foreign barrier, the smell of the creek rich
and suddenly sharp, he tumbled quick
as the rock slide he started to where the water
began, slipped in deep and up for breath

and again down to the jumble and cleft
of stones, every cell in his parched shell
soaking in sweet Piedmont water. He breasted
it upstream for sanity, for food, for his life,

like a woman leaning naked, arms wide
against the push of the current,
and everywhere the water-dripping music
of the wood thrush, sweet, slow.

We grieved too soon after we found
you, still and stunned
on the ground, for
you were stronger

than we could have known. You took what
we offered, put
it to spirit
and feathers. But

(forgive us) you just weren't made right.
We saved you, not
for flight, but for
this still caged air.

Red-shouldered Hawks

I like to think of them using it now
as a weekend retreat, that branching nest
high in the great red oak by the road
where children play late into dusk

now that it's light longer. She's forgiven
him, taken him back. They still wheel
and soar, split the strident air, then sail
off to Taos, perhaps, dual income, no kids

though heaven knows they tried. Twice,
by my count, but the air here is rough
with crows and that first time they foraged away
too long. Again they tried, but April sank hard

into blackberry winter. She called and called
him to take his turn, but he was spinning
through midlife crisis. Keeping eggs warm
takes too much time when you have to save

yourself. Spring warmed at last, he winged home
full of stories and contrition and mulberry wine.

Leaving the nest was hard at first, each day
she tried, fighting an awful gravity freighted
with the pull of planets, whole worlds, spilling

with those first frantic cries, the aching curve
of porcelain against her breast, under her wings.

Next time you see her she won't call
herself Bibby — she'll have mastered the L.
But you don't know that yet, won't know
either how she will tie her shoes, or pull
her wagon, or feed the cat herself. She'll show
you all that, next time you see her,
display what she will wear to church,
and she'll ask where her mother is now.
But you don't know that yet, so you hug
her mother, Cindy, and tell your sweet niece
Next time I see you you'll be so tall ...
and touch her bright

                                      hair sticky and fragrant
with the sea, Cindy's hair when we spent
long cicada summers at Wolf Bay, thirty
years ago. Two brown girls with two
whole weeks, time to fish and float
and we don't have to leave tomorrow
Cindy said, spinning circles in the water
off the pier, *or the day after, or the day
after that,* so much delight, no way
to hold it but to spin and spin, her hair
streaks of light and salt across her face
or the next day, or the next

time you see
Libby you will hold her hand while
they play Amazing Grace and Clair
de Lune but you don't know that yet. Nor
that after the memorial you will tell her
about Wolf Bay. About water that turns
pink at night, about water that sparkles
at night if you stir it up, like when
a child spins in the shallows. You'll take
her hand, Libby's hand, and lead
her slowly, so slow, waiting for her
laugh before you spin her faster and faster
motorboat motorboat step on the gas

The persimmon grove, where the lake
used to be, shook
with autumn, spilled
back grace awhile,

gave way too — one house, then dozens
more, and each green
trunk fell, gone now
for years. No one

remembers the lake. Dragonflies
flashed there, bees, haze —
gray pearlscale fish.
I'm sure of this.

AFTER THE DIAGNOSIS,
I HEAD FOR THE LAKE

and the swallowtails must have just crawled
from their cocoons, look, shivery blackgold
satin wings, barely used, cover the ironweed
and the butterfly bush's rampant purple spread

above the lake churning with Canada geese
here to stay, apparently, blown off course
into the red stain of Piedmont mud
and living on forbearance and bread

crumbs, see, pygmy sunfish and a great
heron stalks, sights, throws himself white
feathers and bones into one jab, then rises
skylit, dripping, surprise as edged with grace

as that late chrysalis shaking on the willow
with wind or something wilder.
                         Barn swallows
stitch the edge of the air to the lake, quiver
the way those nearly-born wings push, heave

their way, as though they know it will work,
through all that tough thread, that tight silk.

Duals

Barely had we got the bamboo under control
before the wisteria started pulling down
the woodpecker tree and the Japanese
honeysuckle began strangling the wild clematis.
We carried armloads of the exotic invaders
to the compost heap, but now, with the first
warming, there they are again, twining
with sweet virgin's bower. It gets me

the way we never can pull them apart for good.
The way (imagine it) while you wait for the doctor
to bring back the report on what he calls *markers*
those signs in the blood he will read for your life
while your gut clenches and you lose your breath
there's somewhere, not in equal measure, don't think
you get equal measure in this, a grain of something
like delight. These days you take what comes

like this odd April, chilled and then too warm,
but the smell of wisteria can take you back
forty years *where a creek bed ran rich*
with roots and ferns, green minnows flashed,
and damselflies, and a girl could find arrowheads
and then the woodpeckers are here, homing
back to their broken tree, and the wild clematis
blooms late this year, but it does bloom, just in time.

ABSOLUTION

When I read the news about the boy from Monroe
who, outraged that his cat had scratched him, threw
the small tabby into the microwave, then heaved
her body, still living, against the trunk of a tree

did the tree flinch? And did whole forests shout?
I found my young cat, soft in a slant of light,
felt the buzz of his start-up purr. That night I pulled
him from his usual bed by my feet, fixed a shawl

around his warmth, settled him down in the place
he always would choose if he could, face to face
and all night I smelled the cat scent of his fur, talc
clean laundry, old lace. All night, rain ticked

against the window. All night, his breath on my face
when I breathed it in, was cool, like the rain, or grace.

LIGHT

Afterward they all said the same thing
every time   the ones who looked down
on this from space   *blue marble*
against the impossible dark nothing
but blue   so fragile you could weep

And we listened   or didn't
and went about our lives   Below

blue widens to woods and farm
livestock scatters   A rattle
of wood ducks rising   A fox bursts
from the brush   coat like flame
Something wrong in the air

pulls the coyote from the scent
of the soil   Soft ears flick once
shining   rimmed with morning
She lowers her head again to the chase

while the ones who flew before tell
over and over again what it was like
the sun out every portal   how the flight
kept them so light that even when they slept
they were floating

Feb. 1, 2003

LITTLE BADGER-BIRD

Even the kiwi's feathers have been
transformed into an approximation
of coarse fur. The barbs have lost
their hooks and each feather, though
fluffy at the base, becomes toward
the top, hard, hair-like, and
waterproof.

        — *David Attenborough*

Sometimes a wing or something like a wing
or wing's memory opens along this reach
of scuttle crabs and starfish, when the beach
wind rises, sharp with petrel cries and salt-stung
spray, and something ancient in your feathers
(that aren't exactly feathers, more like fur,
more like the burrowing animal you are
now) lifts and shivers.

                When did your mother's
mother's mother, lazy with the lush
spill of a world not yet far from grace,
make that choice (that wasn't really choice,
more like the way a small surprise of fish
will swerve into the current when it shifts)
to run only on land?

             Enemies were fewer
then, the earth more generous then for you.
So now all night you stalk the spumy drift
of blown-by sand above the low-tide sound.
Come morning, for your life, you'll go to ground.

AFTER THE STORM,
SOUTH MOUNTAIN STATE PARK

The last day we climbed, my husband and I
up the trail that began at the ranger station

a trail that, where it flattened into a meadow
of lyre-leaved sage, sheltered moccasin flowers

or so we'd been told, deep yellow with brown
curls framing the lips, Zen masters, waiting

for the pull of the sun, the exact distance
of shadow and rain, whatever dropped

from the sky. We pushed through branches,
trunk-span limbs, a creek you could step

across, which we did, searched for hours
with the whiff of carrion from somewhere

and three, four, then a dozen vultures circling.
Finally, done in, we napped on warm stones,

steeped in the mingled fragrance of meadow
and death and a dream of black wings rushing

then woke astonished as, an arm's length above,
one bird, then another and another, brushed past

our faces, a score more in a holding pattern.
We stared for the length of a caught breath

as they wheeled and dipped, then, knowing us
for what we were, veered and lifted away.

JEREMIAD I: THE STARLINGS

After the concert, after the Brahms
and Debussy, the fathoms-deep boom
of bass and cello, glittering arpeggios
like peppered sunlight

after we streamed stunned from the balconies
and galleries of the hall to the parking deck
across the street, garish in halogen glare
we heard them:

Starlings, hundreds of them, shrilling,
as the sun never set there, never a drape
of dark to whisper sleep, shrilling for their lives
their midnight songs.

Although the sky outside my house tonight
reflects all the light of the city, deep night
as lucent as dusk, the trees are quiet.
If a star

should fall tonight we would not know, nor
could we follow it. Not like those seafarers
of old, ready to follow the icy spill
of foreign constellations

across the whole ocean, who, already lonely
for the land they had not yet left,
the hedgerow and the heath, brought on board
their small creatures

sparrows, starlings to keep them company
in the strange world where the land was wild
where the streets were gold and the sun
was always shining

SISTER VIVIENNE, ENDOWED
after a consultation with a friar

The woman on the tractor, the one
who made the abbey gardens shine –
Sister Vivienne, he answered, as he ushered
me into his box room off the refectory.
Endowed, he said, making that gesture,
you know the one I mean.

I have cancer, I said and he turned,
offered me a poem by Saint John
of the Cross, talked of division
within my church, decisions split raw
from the faith he loved, his missions
in Rwanda, *the genocide years*

and nodded me out as a tour bus arrived.
Angel trumpets and butterfly bushes
exploded high and wide, spilling fragrance
when they chose. Bloomed-out hibiscus
towered twice my height, everywhere
the whirr of small things, feasting

and just ahead, the figure of Sister
Vivienne, breasting the deep meadow
grass at the prow of her tractor. In her wake
white egrets, a dozen at least, flapped
and settled, rose again and settled, snapping
up every quick jumping thing.

OTTER SLIDE

I found it at last on Friday, lying beneath
the leading edge of leaf fall, the red clay slicked,
worn to warm mahogany with Briar Creek
water as, legs too slow for leaps of faith

they threw themselves on their bellies to the stream
again and again. I knew it had to be somewhere
near. Young otters had launched months before,
their moving heads each night trailing vees

in the water, pouring off the streetlamp shine.
In a week it would have been too late, the cotton-
woods fast undressing, then the oaks, the fattened
persimmons on the path hiding all sign

of the slide, blanketing all that animal abandon,
warm fur, their secret joy as near flight
as we can understand. I think of them, bright
water ahead, the plunge, then ripples, then none.

AND HOW THE SNOW RETREATS
AND ALL THEY THOUGHT THEY KNEW
OF LANGUAGE FALLS AWAY

The Inuit have a hundred words for *snow*
but none for *robin*, that continental bird,
vanguard of winter's dissolving. Scientists

say they are moving far north now, drawn
wrong by early pushing green,
huge flocks to claim the sagging

tundra and bank against the snow
the soft coals of their breasts.
What terror of delight stirred

in the watchers who track snowy owl
and ptarmigan day by short day, stolid
as ice freezing, to see this bird —

such a wonder — the way it sits upright
in the permafrost among the foreign
tendrils of bracken and fern, how

when the flock rises, nameless, a hundred
brown ash wings opening at once, those
flames, that red, how it singes the air.

WHAT THE BEAST SAID

For starters, you must change your life.
Give up your grief,
what's gone is gone.
Not everyone

knows this yet, but they will. But just
yesterday morning
hawks, the same pair
returned to their

nest in the white oak by the road,
now
in the world, now
gone.
    Change it how?

OTHER POEMS

HEAT LIGHTNING

Morning air stirs vaguely chill, blankets
dragged out, jumbled. Leave the window open.
After all, it feels like spring: white throated
sparrow singing of pure sweet Canada. Listen!
Orange-slash sky. We'll have thunderstorms
by afternoon.

       My big Siamese cat
noses up my length and licks my eyelid
stands on me complaining, claws retracted.
Sometimes he forgets he has them: I have
three scars on my wrist.

       The storm boils dark
from the west. The windows rattle. Close them.
I don't hear the sparrow now anyway. The storm
will strike us, and it will pass, and I
will still be here.

Fear of Heights

He perched, intense and wary, on the fallen
tree that spanned the creek. We leaned so close
we could see his feathers ruffle, see him
shift minutely with the sunlit breezes.

Sunlit — far too early for a barred owl.
Not even twilight yet, but he was wakeful;
and then — what shift in air or scent alerted
the owl to us, entranced upon the clay bank?

He turned: his eyes gleamed hooded, black and slanty;
dazzled with daylight — wild thing — he watched us
above him on the bank, then without effort
he pushed into the breeze — one beat — he vanished.

The bank on which I stand is towering.
Miles below, the water? Rocks? More easily
could that wild thing stand his ground and lock
his eyes with mine, than I can mine with yours.

CHINON

We'll bury you tomorrow.
Somewhere we can plant a tree,
a tree that will breathe
wind back out to wind,
easy, all winter long.

Heart failure, they said,
though no knife will prove it.
And for two days you sucked
air that never was enough
while your body chilled.

Last week, four days
before the invasion
that would break your heart,
I lay in migraine petulance,
you, warm against my inner arm;

your eyes steady, full
of what you kept from me.
Your heart beat sweet and strong.
I pressed deep into your fur,
listening to your breathing.

Muzzie, Stormed Roses

We could not name it
tamp the clay on what she feared
but she knew its face

knew me, knew herself:
"How lucky she has her mind
still, isn't it?" No

she could watch it lurch.
Purpling, bed-exhausted flesh
parched marigold skin.

So proud, grandmother —
"Does she want her pain pill now?"
Nurse adjusts a leg.

"Here's her potty chair."
I turn toward the window, watch
rain pounding on rain

stone patch overgrown
flattened, sodden rosebushes
water with no quench

       sunwarm brownhaired child
       picking roses, stripping thorns
       (careful) from each stem

       under every leaf
       under each bone-china bloom
       where the sweet dew hides

When the rain is done
sparrows slip and flounce again
when the blooms are dry

I will bring roses
cut them deep. With vicious stems.
This time, thorns will stay.

sits on a jellyfish
and now they call him Stinger Butt.
Wide Track catches the hook in his hair.
Wide Track gives up on the sailboat
trudges back up to the porch swing
beyond sound of the shouts of the sailors.
Wide Track reads the Bomba books
by marshfrog symphony.
Down the road, just past the armadillo tracks
where the air hangs still
howler monkeys flounce and scream.

Wide Track keeps killies
in a wide-mouth jar
throws bread to the laughing gulls
that wheel and shriek out of reach
        Wide track, eat a tack
        gonna have a heart attack
Wide Track reads space books
by flashlight.
Just ahead, beyond the gulls
rockets hang clean in shining air
        sailing   sailing

JEOPARDY

Mad Miss Morrison is muttering again
curling her tongue around syllables and spit
as she waters the sasanqua, hissing
at the brown orb spider, the mealy bugs
on the azalea's new leaf.
                              She isn't talking
to them, of course. She's answering
her brother, God rest his soul, cousins
who never write or call. Invective
spills as she walks her terrier with the limp
and the dragon breath under the dogwoods
those blazing transplants from the mountains
the ones that may not survive another decade.

Because I couldn't wait any longer
I whisper out back, fifteen years
after my husband left never wondering
how it started. Because I was Oh Christ
tired. Because it never rained. Because fire
climbed Forty Acre Rock every summer
and we dreamed fire every night, dreamed
northern lights, and aching sweep
of penguins, and a swarm of stars

over mile-deep ice.
                              Where they tell us
now of blasted arrows, tiny squid
like transparent fingers, fragile as oilslick
over still water, baked by a suddenly
fiercer sun
                and we turn and turn
in our own affairs, spilling our words
to dusky sparrows in the hedgerow
answering questions no one has, as yet
thought to ask.

THE SUMMER OF THE TICKS

the dogs at the pound all wore helmets
of brownred mail; eyes crusted, they battled
anemia, on top of all the ordinary kennel ailments.

We brought one home, dipped her
spent hours picking tiny crawling horrors off her face
and around her tail, a dog to save a marriage.

When she killed my cat, she became your dog
and I cried, naked in the bathtub,
hunched over the gash in my belly

now nearly healed. I screamed my hate
for your dog and you and the acts we performed
that would never make a child

that summer, stunned with the ticks bloated
but sucking so deeply from life that they say
the only way to kill one is to set it on fire.

THE SECOND LOSS: NINE YEARS
AFTER THE DIVORCE, AND COUNTING

These days, whenever your memory
nudges surfaceword (a dolphin pup
wary, watching, circles out of reach
tries a roll, grins, and moons the beach)
I invite it right in, sit down for jasmine tea
look straight into its flouncing center
and grin back.

I miss my lovely hate.
It was a brilliant hate.
It sang to me, warmed me
curled round me fragrant as coffee
shaped me into one who lives well without you.
All those names, scratched in sand
gone to sand.

The Bard called it bootless, troubling curse
to fate, so fruitless. Mutely turn the page
instead, and on with it
as I have done, pages turning with the seasons
easy as breathing. But worse
I think, this impish end of it
without the rage.

Those days, I watched the glow go down
certain my delicious hate would wake
past time to catch that same orange brand
wriggle warm into coral long worn to crystal dust
shout like stars in sentry sand spread wide to chalk
the whole greenbright earth
with ancient salt.

You stroll McAlpine Lake with your arms
in tweed, hair under the deerstalker cap
arrogantly brown, like some endangered
teak. In your jacket pocket, Proust
no doubt, or Hegel. You amble in careful
melancholy better suited to someone

my age, for example. Your hunter gloves
sueded like butter, or the skins of those
baby rats Mad Miss Martin fed the python
in seventh grade. Or the graysheened mole
the mower blades kicked up last August

how without a mark on his velvet body
he lay on my boot as limp as Monday.

You take in the water with whatever
is behind your eyes as I pass. I mark
your hair again while you drop back
without seeing me.

PINE VOLES

I find their holes everywhere and see
smoke from some Stygian hellmouth
under every stone. They strike from below,
devour the roots of azalea and spicebush,
corms of Little Sweet Betsy and Catesby's
trillium — doomed, all, though I won't know
for a while yet. I curse, pour poison, replace
the shards of brick, put aside squeamishness,
the small animals' great thirst before dying.
Good riddance I grumble.

          When my father left
that last time, to marry his lover's daughter
I took his attitude: *Send me a postcard.*
He does, from time to time. Once he sent snapshots
of the monkey house at the Jackson Zoo. Once
pictures of his wife's children, and their children.

The game trail at the top of my garden leads
to a hollowed trunk where something solitary digs,
sleeps, leaves its scat. All around the tree odd
seeds from somewhere are sprouting.

The monkey grass is faintly yellow, the first
sign the tubers are sheared clean at the soil
line, the first sign they're back, the voles,
curled in their burrows, their bellies tight
with sweet roots or poison. What's left is that long
slow withering.

RECAPITULATION

Let's say the marriage is on the skids
on the rocks   over   kaput   finis
and you're wondering just how the hell
you plan to live the rest of your life
let alone tonight   and you pray please
please   no words past that please
and it all comes whirling back   the start
his hands   his face   his quicksilver words
and you bargain with God   please God
let him mean it   let it be true
and you know if you can have just this
you'll never ask for anything again
nor need to.

Actaeon, in the Wind

"But to have something like
this... I don't know what's
next..."
        -Naranja resident the morning
        after Hurricane Andrew

He could have saved his breath. Just
a fox hunter passing a wheatgold day
his dogs and his bow, the sun bright
burning on his face, on bracken, warm
enough to shed it all, face up, horns
faintly blowing, there! and away
the wood so full taste of bright wine
whipping his face through brushy spaces
along the fence and over! and then the lake

and she was just there, Artemis, so
sudden, of course he knew the rules
how he wasn't to see her naked, but
you know I couldn't help it, there
you were in front of me moonsilver fire
beauty! not my fault but I am sorry
won't let it happen again and so on
like that until the indifferent sweep
of light across his face, and the arrow
and the hounds and the hounds and

then the horse backing, shaking
his mane, a whicker of wet leaves
moving, just a darkwarm galloping horse
hellbent for home, under the searing moon.

though he should have, God knows
and why he didn't is the God's mercy
after three weeks of frenzied nausea
and Aunt Luanda said he would take
nothing but milk, we stand on the porch
bringing milkshakes to fill the empty

space between his bones and skin parched
and stretched thin as the paperwasp
nests in the shed. *Where's the deer haunch?*
you ask. *Where did all those ferns come from?*
The porch smells of turpentine and new
paint. Dust and sunlight spill through ancient

live oaks out Porter's window, home
he told us a lifetime ago, to wonderful squirrels
a fabulous sport known nowhere else
red and black, white-nosed and fierce.
Luanda lurches from the back room, ushers
us in, wakes mad mute Little Porter

her hunting companion, and Mona, her books
and quilts like moons around her frantic
gravity. *Your cousins,* Luanda cries. The tapestry
curtains swallow the sound. The house
is spotless. *I cleaned it good* she says.
God knows, Porter was bad and if he died

I wanted it nice. For the visitation. Behind her
Porter stands in the door, weakness framing
his face like spent desire. White-throated
sparrows lament *poor sam peabody peabody
peabody.* You touch my neck. I wish I could
show you the squirrels, I whisper. But Luanda

is hurrying us into the back room past
the highboy and all those plates, where a red
squirrel poses on a stained oak board, his starched
rigor as patient as heartwood. His black feet
splay on the mount and his head arches, forever
straining toward some high, perfect nectar

For Wesley Todd, Not My Child

You sleep embracing sleep
night, sweet breathing
arms curve open as you face the sky
that arches over a baby's blanket.
No fetal, self-protective curl
for you, loved baby.

You stand wobbling, slide
baby legs apart
like the mimosa behind you where it forks
you tip forward, tip back
grip tonguetip in your teeth
and let the foam ball fly.

I once had a cat who could balance like that.
Just past college, twenty years gone.
He took my love and a shoebox bed,
dug into sleep like a foxhole.
Nothing to see but furry brown back
curving over bulging cardboard walls.

You shout "Brown! Brown!"
as the plate of warm bread arrives.
Peas pushed aside, corn ignored
you choose a doublehandful of sweet zucchini bread
and, rich with delight in being Wesley Todd
make a meal of it.

I could make a meal of all your choosing.
Gobble each agate (this stone, not that)
picked from the creek. Would gladly gulp
all that holy time for making up your mind
the way I breathe in your skin
while you sleep and breathe out

only wonder:
when did my choice, my chance
first begin to curve
the unthinkable distances
from not just yet
to never?

Gypsy Dance

We burn, swear and pull
our hearts out like rubber bands
tension like gravity demands
release, arms pull together
we resist, hold that tension
as Zoltan instructs us
learning the dance.

Snow piles under the eaves
breath smokes by the furnace
sweat slicks arms, faces
wild Hungarian fiddles whip
music into mania, we spin
until Zoltan says
"take your balance."

Zoltan's hand burns on the silk
of my blouse. My back strains
against him <u>push</u> he commands
me left to right and <u>push</u>
into a spin "on your <u>heel</u>, one, two
<u>now</u>" and spin and spin
and balance is a thunderclap
and gone as quickly.

"Take your balance"
Zoltan says
"make yourself safe."

In the hills of Buda
a gypsy girl flounces, whirls
away from her partner, he stamps
clicks heels together, eyes lock
learning balance.

After you have left me again,
the wine spilled, the words
wrong, but out there to stay
I turn a dozen perfect heel spins
down our polished maple hall
dream of the Danube churning
goldbrown to where the world stops
and the Black Sea sings.

By morning it's back again, shoots
of the bamboo we've already cut flush
with the ground, bundled and hauled
to the curb. It spikes from dirt sucked
clean of grass or brush, full of roots
tangled in rain.

       Our back yard lies bare,
faint sheen of moss only. Moss can live
on nothing, on stone.

          There, another one
lies barely underground, stolons corded
like veins pumping just under the skin
of my wrist, in the bend of my knee
where year by year, purpling spiders
bloom and spill, bleed down my calf,
tumble toward age.

         Saturday we'll try
again, chop and shear, twist string
around wild stiff bundles, spread thick
mulch to feed the newly bare earth
where just below, rising here from dirt
and here, and again here, it pushes
pushes toward the light.

MALLARD CREEK

It's really called Little Sugar
but on this drenched Festival Day
it's full to spill with mallard wind
malachite gleam and paddling
soft push against curling water.

This one rises, all bay breast
and broad, beating wings, churns
the oilsplashed water. He should
have stayed with his harem in deeper
colder places.

        Five hens make spokes
from a concrete half-circle that feeds
sludge and slick to the creek
they dip and strain, dip and strain.

Children powdered with funnel cake
excess point and crouch: "There. Look
there." Mother, turquoise and copper
curving against her throat, watches
the birds suck and suck creek bottom
under the pewter sky.

Sand

for my brother

I've had it, you said when our father
in his sixty-eighth year declared himself
not ready for that grandfather thing
and left the state where you lived
with your astonishing children,
heading for Denver with the daughter
of another lover, the third to take
him in wedlock since he left
our mother and us.
                           He's not worth it
you said when in his seventy-fourth year
he moved back to town, broke
and staggering, and, flailing after
someone to blame, fell upon you
his son, who took him in, risked your job,
arranged the treatments, the therapists,
gave him money to return to Denver
and the wary woman who might still be there.

All I've been doing all these years
he told you *is trying to replace your mother*
and your face closed like the Pied Piper's mountain.

No more: this reckless father whose blood
whirls in your own design. Maybe that's why
you fell weeping to the floor the night
your first son was born, Beth's hard delivery,
this new son, this new father.
                        All our lives
we thought love for him would simply appear
in a panpipe flurry, lead us into grace. Instead
we keep scrabbling for a finger grip in the sheer
mountain face, a trick door out, or, at the least
a cranny somewhere that doesn't run with sand.

56

Climbing

Where the world stops at the edge
of the bay on the rift at San Andreas
you can keep flying straight to Japan
but we stop off and start to climb –
you, grinding through the exams
that will raise you in your profession,
me, fleeing student essays and final
grades, up the muscle-breaking hills
to the sea and Alcatraz beyond.

In Russian Hill long-haired men with arms
like rapiers move through Tai Chi slow
as breathing. On the cable car women complain
when the car turns away from Pier 39
and legendary shopping. In Chinatown
the derelicts bring their cats to nap
beside them as they urge coins
from tourists. This one, crouched
in a deep **salaam**, does not look
at the bill I leave but whispers
thank you, thank you
into the mat. The cat stirs.

After exams and the fog have burned away
we hike the fir-lined trail to the top
of Mount Wittenberg, stoke our energy
with blackberries. And near the top
where redwoods sweep the sky
and the trail rises like a caught breath
the clap of a hundred wings as band-tailed
doves, all at once, seek another tree
and then another, and another,
and still again, leaving us wondering
where they are going, wondering
where the hawk is, wondering

Double Ring: Making the Bed

My lover made it first: this glowing teak
torn from the raindense forest before we paid
attention to such matters, burnished stock
rubbed breathing warm into this thing, this bed

which I make now, in layers, stretch and give
over to it. Sheets fragrant as the kitten
that braves canyons, mountains, in the heave
and toss of linens, crouch, pounce, and flatten

deep in the dark, invisible cat. The aim
is masking wrinkles: my old quilt will block
sagging corners no hospital would claim
haphazard sheets. Paired circles interlock

with all the colors of that jeweled race
(warbler from Cape May, the golden plover)
we lost between the jungle and this place
on their way to winter sanctuary. Ever

since we started we have played this dance
this laying down of layers in a skein
that twists the walls in words to lagging silence
to the way that I forget if I begin

where he leaves off, making it up, trying
out the story. Yes and no sleep together
here, lying alone, or with him, but lying
or not, or him or me, or both, or neither.

After eternity ends this time, you turn
in and down, just the way your ballet
teacher said never do. Ocean-born, you seek
a lower level, pull earth over your head
like the cellar door. Wait for subsequence,
lover or not. Hover still as air
between the panes of windows. Curl
around the part of you that waits
for the longest day of the year
to fly with Alcyone past the long
blowsy grass, through the cedary wood,
along the fernwet path to the sea
spread your wings over the winter solstice.

Insomnia

My libido spends
itself in desire
for the marsh. Mornings
I rise facing west.
Invisible wings beat
in my blood. I stretch
neck, shoulders
to give them room.

The bat skims the marsh
surface   tension
like fine webbing absorbs
then expels us as a film
run in reverse
shows how the inked blotter
returns the ink to the pen

Stunned with stars
and sound
we fly west
and presently east

Against the Wind

An easy mistake – I startled you. You paced
the brickyard, drew on your cigarette, a brigand
in tweed. The winter sun bounced off your face,
your eyes – you saw me then. I stretched my hand
toward you, a gesture anyone might make:
Finish your smoke, I'll wait with you. You reached
for mine, then seeing my intent, pulled back.
Somewhere a second when we might have touched.

Too late for me to reach again, we pressed
into the restaurant against the wind.
It took all the wine, the food, the talk of why
the world is as it is, why we resist,
and why we're never ready before I opened
my fist enough to let the trapped spark fly.

upon reading that for Bosnian
women raped by the victors in
the war with Serbia, and for their
children, the violation *"marks
an end to hope... not even their
families will take them in now..."*
—*The Charlotte Observer*

This one's mother's mother's mother danced
the Zensko Camce before the century
turned, led a bright line of women
along the browngold spill of the Drina.
Turn, lift and hold on one leg, sink
nearly to the ground, barkbrown face
to the sun, sheer stone as the face
of the Velika-Strana.

Because the Turks brook no defiance
it's all part of the dance, her fist
behind her back.
            Women turn, clasped
hands V above the brilliant heads, high, clean
as the sky is when there's no one to fight
except the enemy.

Both sides of the Drina, women beat
kaleidoscope skirts on stones,
leave them to dry as they collect
earth that settles in the sweet clefts
of rock, a pinch at a time
gather it for their lives
into the heavy folds of their aprons,
cherish it home into spilling gardens.

Eurydice Returns to the Realm of Proserpina

"And now I see that I am sorrowful
about only a few things, but over and over."
—Mary Oliver

Did you hear singing when I turned and passed
the place where earth returns to stone? The light
let go, I felt it when it left, but sweet
mercy, the songs, the children, my Orpheus

at the gate, his howls becoming symphonies.
He couldn't help it, he was formed by the music
he created. Do you hear it now? You might mistake
it for the thrush, the river's rushing, minor keys

and percussion. He gave up all he was
to bring me out, but gods, stone and brine,
he failed. You know they tricked him, Proserpina.
That wasn't me he saw ghosting in the glass,

smiling from Acheron. No matter. Please see
me down. I cannot take your hand, that aching
cold you warmed just once by pomegranate
flame. It is enough I see how all your sweetness

will flee this place, when they lift you free for spring,
how I will harden to crystal, how, when the shepherds
fall before the Seraphim, I will ring back the harmony.
You could have been a friend. Touch him for me.

Keep our dances said the man
from that stunned end of the world
Hercegovina. *They're lost
to us* he said. *They belong
to the enemy now, past
the Drina's goldbrown churning.*
And because we can't hold back
all that wilding from children,
women lost, raped, thrown away
we revive their dance. And like
Alice down the rabbit hole

it's easy once you give up
balance, accept limp and sway
as natural. Think heartbeat
with a hiccough, like apple
applegalloping, apple
applegaloping. This off
center dance, easy to learn
till you think what you're doing
and fox-trot, waltz, comfortable
western twos, threes, fours stretch out
catch you up
                like a potion

labeled *drink me*. Like the sand
shark, nosing estuaries
down east, how it swims to breathe,
to eat, everything, when it
tangles in the line washed up
to some creosote piling
and all that surging is down
how it stops, astonished, it
simply stops.

CYNTHY, IN THE CATHEDRAL

I never learned to finger *Clair de Lune*.
When Cynthy and I played four-hand piano
our skills ran more to *Chopsticks, Heart and Soul*
camp songs, *Kum-Ba-Yah*. And when my hands
strained toward Debussey, it wasn't moonlit
simplicity, but sealocked cathedral that
compelled me. Oh, it had too many notes
for me to reach, but I learned how to fake it.
And after Cynthy turned from our duets
and into arabesques melting to moonlight
I pounded that engulfed cathedral skyward
I played it freighted with the pull of planets
into the air so just one day, one minute
it flashed into a world that did not waver
then sank beneath the sea. With me, without me

When Cynthy died they wove the *Clair de Lune*
within, around the stands of rose and lily
dying as we breathed them by the chancel.
But I can't breathe in the moonlight. When my fingers
ache to pound some living music home
again I seek the seadepth for that chapel.
Again my hands are short the reach of music.
Again I fake it. Hands splay out like talons
over the harmonics, fingers cramp
with holding down keys by the edges, seven
notes at once. This time the music pounds
me from the heaving pressure of those fathoms
into the sear of light, the rage of music
sucks me off the soft pedal, the music
shoves me, will me nill me, through the walls.

Before the doctor
where, despite the good diet and sound
living, never mind the Nautilus
my heart started fluttering out
of control, before the rush
of blood, and their hiss or whine
or other ruckus (there must
be a noise for what it does
reading and scribing the peaks
of my heartbeat)
before all that

there was this blackbird
oilslick colors slipping
from wings and throat still warm
piled by the hedgerow
and as I reached down
expecting the feathers
it turned to what it always was
gills of mushroom capsized, steaming

like the wet leaf floor
of some first forest
where, after the doctor
I would turn
to my pleasures
heedless

as the kitten
too long kept inside, safe
stalking a mole cricket wall to wall.
I watch how he circles and feints
pushes the Indian rug into peaks
to hide behind
how the world becomes a rush
of stream on stone, moss
and all those holy ferns
how finally he pounces
feathers at his tongue.

My Neighbor Hunts Squirrels from Her Kitchen Window Blind

It's for the birds and all those rich seeds
thieved from the feeders she does it, you
know — and for the blue

promise of her water feature.
She can drop each plush raider
with one shot to the head

usually, and the small gray
corpse is often gone by
morning. That's why

she has the best
birds in town, a feast
for the eyes.

LOVE POEM

When I'm behaving well and you're not
even trying, it's easy to romance
little things, moving through halls
just so, charged though your glance
never leaves your book.
                                        I've got
an idea you enjoy it, this dance
we do in doorways, at the walls
in words, in legendary silence.
At this point, I don't know what
to do with you, so I rinse
the dishes, water the plants.

Sleep Paralysis

I'm afraid it will happen
again, that sudden fall, stunned
into stasis. When prick-ends
of dreams tease my fingers and
lips, and blood pools behind my
eyes, it's already too late,
no way out, mouth like a carp
sucking air that never is
enough, hands still as granite
push air freighted with the pull
of planets

         over to you
no more distant than the sheet's
thickness. You could sleep so lightly
I could wake you with one sound,
one jerk awake, but it holds
me down, this fierce gravity
of sleep. Inside this body
I guide my dreams, they circle
like constellations, pulling
me out where there is no air
at all. Wake this body. Wake
me. Wake me.

GOLDFISH EXHIBIT AT THE
TRAPHOLT ART MUSEUM
a found poem from The Charlotte Observer, 2/15/00

The art display at the small museum
      in western Denmark features ten goldfish
            each swimming in its own blender

            Each blender can be turned on
      depending on the viewer's whim
Two fish were blended at the opening

The display, which opened Friday, has caused
      outrage among animal rights activists and drawn
            unusually large crowds to the art museum

            Police ordered the plugs pulled after the Union
      for the Protection of Animals complained. Five
more fish were blended on Sunday

            An investigation
            is under
              way

Small Robin, Unfeathered

Who'll make his shroud?
I, said the beetle,
With my thread and needle,
I'll make the shroud.
                    "The Death and Burial of Cock Robin"

You fell from your nest and came to mine,
such as it was, that flight cage upholstered
with branches and bracken, with soft worn
towels and leaves and a flowerpot bed.

Two days past fledging, you trusted
badly when, exhausted, you placed
your faith in a clumsy-footed slave
to gravity. We try but can never bear

the delicacy of your kind for long, slight
bones, inner mysteries, feathers! Without food
you took to the ivy-clad poplar that first night,
woke parched and famished, cried all day and flew

and flew: this tree, that tree, *come up to me come up*
come up and bound to the soil I did what I could,
called in my language, and by the next day
with nothing to lose you sailed to the stoop and waited

for what would come, let me feed you. Now, *oh, yes*!
you flew to my shirt, my shoes, quivering *feed me feed me*
and I stoked you with worms, cat food, blueberries,
water on an ivy leaf. And then that confluence:

my day's urgent occupations, your small
voracious need. One more worm: I reached
and stumbled, just as you in aching trust
flew to the place my foot would occupy

less than a second, till it felt the terrible softness
warmth, feathers, the ebb of you. The baby coal
red feathers under your throat, your funny robin
squeak. So. The yards are full of robins now,

their breasts afire and nothing I can understand.
They sing all day.

CAMPING AT STONE MOUNTAIN

Nursing a pulled hamstring and a glass
        of wine, I waited for the others to return

from the summit bald. *Take pictures*
        I had entreated, and hobbled to the creek

to read, when a frenzy of yellow and black
        pulled me from my book. Swallowtails

dozens of them, three, four deep, swarming
        a few inches of sand near the water.

With any disturbance they lifted and settled,
        lifted and settled. I crept close, sniffed

the ground for some spilled sweetness
        dusty wings at my nose. *Urine*

my companion clarified late that night
        over beer and stew. *Butterflies*

have nasty habits. Deep night, past the
        time the katydids stilled, a snort, a bellow

repeated again and again as deer marked
        their passage, blew their breath against

the ozone-warm air of the Great Smokies
        calling butterflies

No need to recoil, sir, I'm no
threat to you. The wing? Yes, well,
they all ask that. You didn't hear
about my sister, then. How
just before they touched the torch
to the kindling, Elise at the stake, but her
ruined hands free

she threw the capes over my brother —
swans and me, shone pure, and saved
herself. She wove mine last, didn't finish
in time. I was more swan than the others
in any event. They being older stayed men
longer. Oh, it was harder at first, the wing
pulling me to air

all the time, me anchored by these big feet
and the smell of the soil. The others?
They've moved back into their lives. One
studies the old arts. Three teach. All
have taken wives. Elise stays in the house
most days and will not weave again,
but damn it, sir

didn't she know how much I'd miss the air?
This wing knows, and that's God's truth.
This wing says *Remember?* This wing
says *The sun was yours, and the falling
and the ecstasy of both.* Well, good day
to you, sir. Keep the wind in your face
when you lift off.

THE PRESIDENT'S LADY POSTPONES LITERARY SYMPOSIUM IN FEAR OF POETIC WAR PROTESTS

But my dear, they were
poets. Have you heard
of such a thing? I had
known the word

poet, of course, but I
was thinking more
the air is full of sunlight
and the flag is full of stars

that sort of thing.
Something somebody
wrote about being
fit for yourself to know.

Not this, under rugs, in
the walls, how they snap
at me, poets in the sink, even.
Believe it. I set traps

everywhere, bedrooms,
Oval Office, West Wing.
I caught just one, but
he was singing *be the best*

of whatever you are, be
a bush if you can't be a tree
so I took him to
the park and let him go.

Denial

I think she may not fully accept
how serious this is
my husband told our therapist
about my illness.
And after our good
shrink spoke about the difference
between hope and denial
after we shared notes
on Viktor Frankl's
survival in Auschwitz
after we stopped
my husband and I
for post-therapy cappuccino
eyes meeting astonished eyes
we turned, as we always
do, to the garden.

Sometimes all there is to do
is turn to the garden.
Stones to lay, wildflowers
to set out, damage
to assess and rectify —
Exotic ivy invading the natural
bed, a poplar branch crushing
the lady fern, the white
trillium drooping, sheared
at the base. I slit
the stem, place it in water.
By morning it has lifted
triune leaves, flower reaching
again for the sky.
It will grace
our mantel for days.

A hawk day, clean and full as first
grace, as we pushed
west with our fears.
She has just hours,

they said. *Hurry.* Jean loved hawks, knew
sharpie, Coopers,
and overhead
that red-shouldered

fledgling bent for home, like a car
chasing an hour
as if we might
get there in time

in memory of Jean

When the rain clears
the forecast is *dense fog*

but a great blue heron
emerges   like a muse
if a muse had feathers
and worried about his next
meal   hunched
on the only rock the swollen
creek hasn't claimed

intent on the mudbrown
swirl around him   where just
there   maybe   or there
small fish lurk

or not   He would move
but the rock is dry and just
big enough   and the fog
is   everywhere

RETREAT AT MEPKIN ABBEY

Expect nothing, they told me.
Leave it all at the gate.
Find whatever you need here, books, feelings.

Expect everything.
The moss-heavy oaks, the rocks
to the waterfront, the terraced cemetery
and gardens, a fast hot walk from your cottage. Health.

Expect nothing.
The tang of cabbage soup
so good you laugh out loud.
Wild turkeys, a dozen at least, out
your window chuckling: *this   this   this*

Expect everything.
Miracles. The Holy Spirit in the drops
of water that strike your hair at the end of the Compline.

Expect nothing.
Alligator breasting the Cooper River, low bellows
all night. The tears you can't hold back at Mass.
Swallowtails, hundreds. Herons, silent in flight: *now now*

Expect everything.
The friar you will speak your fears to.
The brother who will serve you bread.

Expect nothing.
And your feet draw silence from the stones
and the stars come out.

Expect everything.
Life. Tomorrow.

THE HERP TRADER AT THE
RED BARN FLEA MARKET

keeps his tiniest sliders
the ones a quarter across
or smaller together in a wide
bowl. One of those fifties

neon green palm trees swirls
up from the middle and seven
sliders shingle its plastic beach.
A dozen spiny softshelled turtles

push and push at the bottom,
as though they know it must
be there, the sand, some phantom
shelter, sweet cover, their necks

(they know it) just long enough
to reach air.
                    Later we walk,
my husband and I, the rain past,
to the creek loud with birds

and running full again. I hold
my fears in with both hands
and watch water flecked
with light and foam, sand

like brown sugar, flooding
the rushes and sedge at the edge
of all I know. They're there
the turtles, I know it, buried

deep in fine sugar sand, their nose-
flute snouts just above the surface
little reeds holding still in the grace
of sweet red-clay Piedmont water

I feel as pregnant women must,
the event fast
approaching — still,
I'm not with child

and never will be. You can't tell
this thing I hold
from ambition,
even rage. None

you could so easily define
as that. What's mine
will outlast grief.
Will change my life.

THE WATCHERS
Beslan, September 2004

Afterward, astonished, they said the same thing,
the watchers, the ones who didn't die, how the sky

suddenly bumped with balloons, all colors pressing
the sharp blue of the fine first day of school. It's what

to do on that good day, carry bright skins and wind
lighter than air. Afterward, the watchers told how it was

when it started: how thick as blossoms the balloons pushed
into the sky as (*those guns*) the children were forced inside

to parch, to wait, and, stunned beyond the strength of small
fingers on the strings, all at once, they let go of everything.

(UNTITLED)

A fall, and no phone, no one to call
and he waited, my gentle cousin,
all the long February night on the damp
garage floor until a friend next morning
missed him at Rotary Club and stopped by.
His vision gone after an assault
a decade ago, his bones badly healed,
he slipped in and out of focus with this world.
Pneumonia set in. He lasted two days.

My family is becoming so small
my mother cried, ragged with tears,
counting up losses, a daughter, a sister,
a husband, a dozen friends, and this
sweet cousin.

Nutbrown hair blown back in the Studebaker.
New-married and on her way to a plum
job in the Bay Area.
She was hearth and woman and
home from the hill, he said she was *what the war
was for,* this stranger she had married
in her South of camellia and honeysuckle.
A husband who wouldn't stop for her amazement
for the wheeling southwest hawkwing
or majesty of boulder and canyon
and who, when he reached the highway
that would lead them into San Francisco,
turned north and kept driving, kept driving
to Seattle and his parents, years ahead
but she wouldn't know that yet, driving her
into the rest of her only life.

ESSAYS AND STORIES

Prayer for the Odd Ones

Say it's a hot Mississippi summer and you're eleven,
just about to slip into the sixties – though nobody will call it
the sixties in just that way for a while yet – and your mother
tells you you'd had polio when you were two, that other
summer when the decade changed and nobody had
television. And Brother Barnett and the entire holy Main
Street Methodist congregation spent all night praying for you,
and in the morning you'd broken your fever and now here
you are, eleven, without a trace of a limp or halting breath
(except for the pesky hay fever) and she tells you how silly she
had been to panic like that, there hadn't been any need for all
those prayers after all: You were going to be fine.

I was. We all were, actually – we were fine, though
we heard the hushed stories about iron lungs, and saw the
pictures.

But we all had to face the needle vats. Every year the
enormous nurses with the leg-of-mutton arms and the white
coats would take over the cafeteria at F. B. Woodley School
for a whole morning, standing over giant pots of syringes
simmering in steamy water, inoculating us, one child at a
time, one class at a time. (It was two years before Sabin Oral
Sundays, with the vaccine-laced sugar cubes we'd let melt in
our mouths, at least ten before *sugar cube* would take on an
entirely new meaning.)

Some of us had to be held down. Some of us didn't. But
afterward we would put our heads down on our desks and let
the tears leak out until the 2:50 bell.

This was, after all, sixth grade, when bravery in the face
of a needle didn't matter if you wore thick glasses, or if your
father was alcoholic.

Every class had its grotesques. Fourth grade had the twins, Lisa and Treesa, fat and frizzy, with tiny mouths and voices like nightingales. They'd make you shiver, those voices. Fifth grade had immense Deborah (who pronounced her name *deBOHRah*) who could crack the stone wall outside the cafeteria and, it was rumored, once did. We had blind Bruce and Albert the albino, whose milky eyes would twitch slightly and constantly while he talked to you, the subject of endless horrified speculation about what it would be like to kiss him.

But you didn't need to be grotesque to take upon yourself the role of *target*. All that was required was that you be *odd*. Like Olivette, who by combination of genetics and poor barbering possessed a bowl of impossible frizzy curls that bounced when she ran, and was freckled so densely and darkly that the freckles merged into spots, like a little wildcat. She would spit like one, too, when Bart Hinson would start in on her.

Bart would take a custodian's damp mop out to recess and, using the strings, would knot a dozen playground pebbles into the mop head. Then he'd zero in on Olivette and run at her, shouting

The freckle-faced running mop
Is Olivette the Odd ...

Until somehow Olivette would either find a teacher or, unencumbered by mop, outrun him.

My oddity, my mark of separateness – for the time being, at least – was the tuberculosis.

Not that I even had it. Dad did. And after he spent six months at the TB sanatorium outside Wiggins, he was fine. We children were, too – Cindy and Larry and I – X-rays and blood tests demonstrated that every month. We didn't mind the X-ray machine, though the plates were cold and it was hard to hold your breath, but the needles took some getting used to. Gentle, flaxen Cindy was the best about it all. Larry bawled, but as he was the youngest, and the boy at that, nobody was surprised. *Baby.* As the oldest, I had something to prove. I pretended I was a captive maiden, facing hideous ordeals, and I always hoped some young man reading a magazine nearby would notice how bravely I held out my arm for the needle, and ignore my glasses. But we were fine, as it always turned out.

That didn't matter. *Waite Bacteria,* Bart Hinson would hiss in science class. Never mind that his father was a doctor; who needs facts when you've got a biological weapon like that? *Waite Bacteria.*

I didn't really care. Bacteria were cool. We had looked at some water from Gordon's Creek under the microscope in Mad Miss McGorkle's class, and the protozoa had neat shapes. They twitched like Albert's eye, only not as fast. They were about like bacteria, I figured.

Mad Miss McGorkle assigned reports on deficiency diseases and read us poetry, sitting on her desk and declaiming, with no notes, the one about the burglar boy who came to rob a house. When in the last stanza *the dame came in,* and she *took out her teeth, and the Woolworth's eye, and the hair from off her head,* we giggled in delight. (*Harr from off her head,* Mad Miss McGorkle said.) And when the burglar boy, facing marriage, shouted, *Woman, shoot!* we rolled on the floor.

And why not? On the bus ride home, we'd open the windows and blast the neighborhoods with endless

variations on the story of "Catalina Matalina," whose feet
were as large as a bathroom mat; who had four teeth in her
mouth, two pointing north and two pointing south. That
was when it was okay, too, to sing songs in the cafeteria
about the cannibal king with the big nose-ring and the
dusky maiden he loved. Nobody cared because every face
in school was white.

The badge of tuberculosis held up, and I wore it
proudly, on into junior high when I plunged into a new
level of oddness. It all came out when we were rehearsing
for the Easter pageant at Main Street Methodist, singing
about how Christ was borne across the sea, *with a glory
in his bosom that transfigures you and me*. When we got to
that part, Jim Ed in the tenor section poked me with the
Methodist hymnal, and all his vermin tenor friends started
to snicker.

They knew. *They knew*. It wasn't my fault the way just
one grew in that year, and how when I dressed out for gym
I was a little lopsided. It's not as if the left one was that big
— it's just that it was the only one I had. The next year the
right one made an appearance, more or less, but the left
one stayed slightly bigger. When my best friend, Carol, and
I devised names for all the parts of ourselves we couldn't
ask our mothers about, we called them the Atlantic and the
Pacific. The left one was always the Pacific. Our bottoms
were our South Americas. Central America and North
America continued our personal geography on around and
up the front.

Carol must have told. Carol, my bosom friend,
friend of my bosom. We had looked up *bosom* in the
dictionary the year before to figure out just what that

90

phrase meant. Did it mean you loved your friend's bosom? Or maybe you were friends when you got bosoms?

We never did figure it out, but as it turned out it didn't matter. A chink in a seventh-grade best friendship will loom as large as the hole in the wall DeBORah cracked. You can pray for two bosoms that look the same; but you don't, because the doctor says you'll even out pretty soon; God doesn't need to get involved.

But you do summon some pretty good prayers for Carol.

EXOTIC ANIMALS AND THE "DOORSTEP" SYNDROME

I went back to Orange Beach this summer for the
first time in five years. And it all seemed just the same
– the old cabins with names like the Honeymoon and
the Bayview, the oyster shell path down to Wolf Bay, the
creosote-smelling piers, the scrub pines that grow right
down to the water, the roots that will gouge a toe if you're
not careful picking your way through the shallow water to
the inlet.

But when I stood where the inlet used to be, where
a canal had been dredged to create more waterfront
property, I saw that something delicate, almost
unnoticeable, had changed and it was a bigger change than
those high-end waterfront homes, and it hit me harder
than the three-o'clock sun.

The mollies were gone.

I remembered the afternoon I'd first seen them.
Then, as now, the air was hot and still and loud with cicada
buzz. The brackish water of the bay was barely moving. The
tide should have been on its way out at that time of day,
but it wasn't. "Nip tide," the old fisherman had told me
between casts. "It'll stay up, oh, all afternoon." The water
lapped up onto the roots of the pine and cypress only when
the long, slow wake from a barge made it to shore.

I saw the first mollie by accident. I had been nosing
around stumps and staubs with my little hand-net, trying
to scare up some baby shrimp for bait, when I saw just the
suggestion of light blue and salmon flickering around a
stump: a fish going after the brown-green algae that covers
just about everything in the bay.

I didn't know it was a mollie at first. There were plenty of other small fish in the bay — menhaden making their tight circles close to shore, baby mullet skipping across the water near the pier, diamond killifish sparkling with their white-edged fins. A green sailfin? The ones I'd seen in the pet stores hadn't nearly that much color...

But when the little fish lifted a remarkable dorsal fin and quivered so that the sun slanting through the shallow water shattered on him, I was convinced he was a male mollie. He darted into the deeper water, startled by my shadow.

Now, I'm a grown woman with a job and bills and responsibilities and all that. But I'd never gotten over the fantasy that had followed me through all those childhood beach vacations — myself as intrepid explorer of uncharted islands, seeker after strange and beautiful wild creatures. With the flickering of salmon and green and blue, it all came back, slamming me like the sun.

Nothing to do but to follow it through: back to the cabin for another net and pail, sunscreen and insect repellent. I had a large brackish aquarium at home. I could take care of a mollie or two.

Catching them, of course, was a different story. My fantasy had always had me enticing the shy, graceful creatures to my hand; it hadn't included those net-eating roots! But in the end, the difficulty didn't matter that much. As long as I sat perfectly still, up to my waist in soft-lapping water, the little fish would swim within a foot of me.

And what came to me as I sat and watched was this: These lovely, wild creatures were *ours*. This was not Borneo or a South American jungle; this was on the coast of south

Alabama. Several hundred yards away, berry-brown kids yelled and splashed, jumping off the pier, trying to avoid sea nettles. Back in the Bayview, someone was frying up croaker and green trout, putting on the pot for a mess of blue crab. Heedless, these little jewels would grace the sunroom of a collector from Brunci – but they were ours.

When I finally caught my pair of mollies it was due less to my intrepid explorer skills than to chance. The sun had long since set. The little fish, dozy in the dark and confused by my lantern, simply swan into the pail.

It would take a couple of days to acclimate these wild fish to my brackish tank, but they would adapt successfully. It would take a while to convince them that the thawed bits I dropped twice a day into their holding tank were good to eat – but they would learn, and eat and grow fat. None of that was the point as I lugged the plastic pail back to the cabin at midnight, mosquitoes black on my arms, my lantern fading and blacking out because I had dropped it one too many times into the water.

The point was simply that they were there, green, salmon and blue, unaware of the kids or the pier, heedless of shrimp boats or pleasure boats; just flaring their fins and flicking their tails and finding enough algae among the roots to keep them for generations.

Ipods. GameBoys. 24-hour movie channels. Children spending bright spring days inside. It's too depressing to think about these, so I'd like to tell you what it was like for a girl to grow up in the '50s, when there was just one channel, and Ike's smiling face shone in the moon.

Close your eyes.

Wendy and Sherry, popping tar bubbles on Rainbow Circle. It's a perfect day for it, a hot August noon sucking gas up into the bubbles until they're tight as a tick, then a quick overcast to keep the tar from sticking to their feet. The best ones pop like bubblegum, sharp and quick, and the girls show each other their biggest prizes just before stomping them.

Wendy, long hair and thick glasses, the cat-eye kind with jeweled rims, has just turned nine. Sherry won't be nine for 21 days yet. It's fun to flaunt that extra maturity, but eight-year-old Sherry points out how her face is softer and smoother than Wendy's.

"You can just tell," she says. "A person can tell. I'm younger."

Sherry's hair is all fluffy curls, and she wears little jump suits because she likes the way her legs look in them. Wendy knows this because Sherry has pointed out that she has the kind of legs boys will soon be whistling at. Sherry sometimes does the bicycle exercise lying on her back in the front yard, while Wendy tries to do a walkover. She never can quite walk over, though, and always has to put both feet on the ground before pulling back up with a little grunt. Sherry can do a walkover, and she never grunts.

Rainbow Circle — the best quartz bits are always pressed into the tar from hundreds of car tires, but they can prize the stones up if they can find a flat, sharp piece of flint, which isn't hard. Sometimes they raise an agate, breathtakingly lightweight, and must break it open in case — oh, yes — there are crystals inside. Usually there is just sand, but once Wendy broke an agate that scattered crystals all over Miss Hayes' driveway.

Miss Hayes is to be avoided. She will chase them off in the space of a shout: "Girls! Get off my driveway. Get out of my yard. Now!" But the fact is, Miss Hayes has the only concrete driveway on the block, so where else are they going to break rocks? They keep coming back, on the chance of more sparkling star rocks and swirly moon rock — rocks too beautiful to have formed on earth — and keep a lookout for Miss Hayes' French twist in the window.

Afterward they will cut through the apartment construction site where the sandy loam has been deeply turned, and pick up three or four flint points apiece. They don't know the spearheads are special and will play with them until they are, inevitably, lost.

Finally, it's down the culvert and under the wisteria that tangles up both concrete sides, stopping to break off a few fuzzy mouse-shaped seedpods, then down to the pond. It's really just a drainage ditch but Wendy and Sherry see potential jungle splendor here, and have been planting ivy and ginger around it, and stocking it with mosquito fish and killies.

"I think it *was* a jungle," Sherry says. "Back before they built Hattiesburg."

"So there might have been tropical fish in it," Wendy adds. Both girls keep aquariums.

"I think those are guppies." Sherry points to
the mosquito fish. "They just don't have much color in
Mississippi."

The fish are doing fine; they don't care about the oil
and mats of algae, and they like the daphnia and mosquito
larvae for lunch.

And today a dragonfly is buzzing over the little pond,
back and forth, back and forth. There. Clear proof. This
was a wild place. It would be nice to have something other
than concrete to sit on, though.

When they leave, honeysuckle weighs the air
with fragrance, and fat raindrops sizzle on the concrete,
blooming with ozone and tar. Fireflies have just started
winking in the grass, and the tar bubbles have congealed
so a girl can walk barefoot back home and have very little
muck to scrape off. Parents prefer that, when they have
oriental rugs in the living room.

"We can get the umbrellas out and make a tent,"
Sherry says. "We'll get a flashlight and watch the worms
crawl up the grass."

"It's really going to storm, I'll bet," Wendy says.
"Let's use three umbrellas."

Dusk falls. Heat lightning flashes, again and again.
Wendy and Sherry, sitting damp and warm in the dark,
waiting for the flood. Breathing. Waiting. Humid little-
girl smells. Sherry smells like sweat and Doublemint
and something tangy, like a nasturtium. It's kind of nice.
Wendy sniffs her own arm and scratches a mosquito bite.

"When will the worms come?" Wendy asks.

"When it gets too wet for them in the ground."

A few more raindrops spatter, and the thunder grumbles off to the west somewhere and fades. The girls push the umbrellas aside and lie in the grass for a while, watching for shapes in the clouds. But they're scudding too fast for shapes to last long, and Wendy has her mind on other things.

Sherry found the best arrowhead. But I still have the Star Rock. Sherry has better legs. But she didn't know what the 'universe' was that time and I did. And Sherry can do a walkover...

The grass is itchy and the girls sit up.

"Listen," Wendy says. Unmistakable, the chugging sound of the bug sprayer. Sure enough, they see the headlights, the truck, the white cloud of DDT, the four little boys on bicycles, racing right in the middle of the stream. Wendy doesn't like to smell it, so the girls stand and stretch.

But I for sure know those mosquito fish aren't guppies!

The girls fold up the umbrellas and head inside. NBC awaits, and ice cream.

A DIARY OF PEPYS
Chronicle of a reluctant hummingbird rehabilitator

Wednesday morning, Sept. 6
Pepys is on patrol. His little body is on high alert, and he
swivels his head, flicking his tail and wings with each turn.
He's intensely focused and loaded for fruit flies. I've just
released a dozen or so into his flight cage, and he knows it;
when some of them fly to his quadrant of the cage he buzzes
his wings and bullets after them, here, there, this branch,
that one, each buzz accompanied by his funny, urgent little
squeak-squeak. He's pure hummingbird. A far cry from the
pitiful morsel he was thirteen days ago...

Wednesday evening/Thursday morning, Aug. 23-24
Pepys came into our lives in a budgie cage, which the
Samaritan who brought him into my husband's veterinary
hospital had stuffed with leaves, twigs and flowers. The
Samaritan had found him lying in her front yard, near death
from hunger and apparent premature eviction from his nest.
My husband put little stock in his chances for survival, but
syringe-fed him 50 percent glucose solution, covered his
cage, and went home for the night, fairly sure that he'd come
back in the morning to find a tiny corpse. But the next day
the little rubythroat was still alive, so Jonathan decided to do
everything possible to give him a chance.

Providing that chance fell to me, as Jonathan (who knows me
so well!) probably had known it would. He'd telephoned me
that morning, asking whether the PerkyPet Nectar I put out
in the yard contains any vitamins or minerals. (It doesn't.)
Knowing hummers' need for protein, we set about to create
a mixture that the little guy would eat. Yogurt whey? He

rejected it out of hand. But the young hummingbird greedily took A/D prescription food for kittens and puppies, mixed one-to-three with the glucose solution. So he was getting some protein and nutrients, though certainly not in the proportions hummingbirds require. Still, it was a start.

Friday, Aug. 25
The hummingbird is still alive, and frantic for food. I feed him every 15 minutes, alternating the PerkyPet with the kitten food mix. I spend far too much of my work day on the phone and on-line... trying to find a source for NektarPlus, a complete hummingbird diet I've read about... trying to find someone in the area who specializes in rehabilitating hummingbirds... trying to find out hummers' schedule – are they supposed to be migrating yet? (Yes, they are.)

I finally reach a wildlife rehabilitation expert in Rock Hill, South Carolina. She tells me first off that I've got to get Pepys out of the budgie cage: The wire will ruin his feathers. That's the least of his problems right now but I locate an old Post Office letter box made from a translucent white plastic cardboard material (to let a little more light in). It has cut-out handles on both sides the right size for attaching a feeder. (If only the little bird could use a feeder right now.) I put a T-shirt on the bottom, a couple of differently-sized branches for perching, and hang a syringe full of glucose/ kitten food mixture plus a feeder full of PerkyPet on the side.

He won't search out food on his own, but when I hold the syringe or the feeder up to him he sticks his little bill right into it and tongues the nectar out. He's got a healthy appetite. But he now seems disinterested in the kitten food mixture.

Saturday-Sunday, Aug. 26-27
Pepys definitely won't take the kitten food mixture anymore. Period. No matter how hungry he must be, he scrambles from one side of the box to the other when he sees that syringe approaching. But he scarfs down the PerkyPet.
So he's getting only sugar water now. Not good. Back on-line, and by hook, crook and link I wind up on the message board for virtualbirder.com, where I find a posting about NektarPlus. I e-mail the author, and discover she's a hummer rehabilitator from Hillsborough, N.C., specializing in avian nutrition, with all kinds of doctorates. Things are looking up.

She suggests a product called Tonic I (for insectivores), distributed by Nekton, the same company that makes NektarPlus. I order that; meanwhile Jonathan has ordered a different nutrition supplement. We've got to get protein into him; as my Hillsborough mentor, Janine, e-mails me: Even a few molecules are better than nothing.

I completely clean Pepys' box every night. He urinates all the time, and the feeder drips; the T-shirt quickly becomes soggy. Pepys needs a dry T-shirt, because in the evening he likes to get off his branch and nestle into the folds of the cotton to sleep.

Monday - Tuesday, Aug. 28-29
The supplement Jonathan ordered has arrived. It's called
Emeraid II (for sick birds), distributed by Lafeber, out
of Illinois. We mix it about one-to-six with the glucose
solution. Pepys sticks his bill practically up to the nostrils
into the syringe and drinks a long time. He loves it.
Thank God.

Pepys doesn't seem to know yet what his wings are for. He
tries to climb from twig to twig in the box, and frequently he
loses his balance and falls onto the T-shirt. He climbs back
up by hooking his chin over the branch, swinging his little
feet up under him, and pulling up.

Pepys needs a bath. Not surprisingly, what with our
struggling to get the kitten food mixture into him, and his
struggling to avoid it, some of it has dribbled down his
breast, and there are dabs on his head and over his eye. Mist
him, use warm water, dry him carefully, Janine writes. So
with considerable trepidation I warm the water in a small
plant mister, lift Pepys who's sitting on a twig out of the box,
and, very gingerly spritz him. He ruffles his feathers, and for
the first time that I've seen, buzzes his wings. If I'd thought
he was trying to get away, I'd have been wrong, because in
the next instant he buzzes again and takes a flying leap right
into the spray of water. He tries to bite the next spritz, sticks
his bill into the nozzle, and finally tries to perch on top of it.
This is fun!

Now I've got to dry my soaked little bird. I carry him on his
twig over to a small 40-watt desk lamp and hold him near it

while I fluff his feathers with a makeup brush. As I lift and
brush, one feather at a time, he fluffs and shakes himself a
little. He seems to enjoy it, so I carefully fluff the feathers
on his head and face. He turns his head this way and that,
even lifts his head slightly when I fluff under his chin.

While Pepys is drying I take advantage of the opportunity
to look carefully at every inch of him. Some of his feathers
seem a little ragged. Could he still be going through his
molt? I'll have to check into that. He has a tiny bald patch
under his chin, right over his crop. Early trauma? His bill
is 3/32 of an inch long (based on that, and the condition of
his feathers, Janine estimates his age at two-and-a-half to
three weeks). He has a coal black jabot under his chin — not
a speck of ruby throat yet. He is absolutely beautiful.

I put my face right down to him, and inhale deeply. He
seems to have no scent at all. He turns his tiny head and
investigates one of my nostrils with his bill.

Wednesday-Friday Aug. 30-Sept. 1
Now that Pepys has learned to buzz his wings, he does it
all the time, exercising his muscles. He lifts his chest and
belly from his branch, buzzes, then settles back down on the
branch, fluffing himself. Clearly, it's time for flying lessons.

We take his box into the back yard where there's an open
space for practicing. We lift him on his little branch and
hold him a foot or so in the air. He buzzes once or twice,
then arches way up, gives a little push and sails a good foot

and a half, landing on the ground. I place my hand, palm up, beside him and he climbs into my hand, using his chin for extra leverage. He settles into my palm and fluffs.

We do this several times, giving him plenty of nectar between flights. By the time he gets tired he's built up to about 10 feet. But he's still crash landing head over tail. And there's not the slightest indication that he's getting any lift at all.

I'm surprised at how much heat his little body generates. He's so little and delicate I guess I'd imagined he'd feel cool. But he feels like a soft little coal in my palm.

Meantime the Tonic I has arrived, and I wonder how to switch Pepys over to it. We mix it one-to-six with the glucose, and he takes it immediately. No problem.

Insects, however, are a problem. In the wild he'd eat several hundred a day, so we've got to scare up some for him to practice on. Naturally, the aphids I've been fighting on my roses all year have disappeared. We'll have to try to get some fruit flies.

Saturday-Sunday, Sept. 2-3
If Pepys is to get enough exercise to start actually flying, he's going to need more space. Jonathan and I decide to convert an old cage I've been using to protect delicate plants into a flight cage, measuring about five feet by three feet by two feet. It's made with hardware cloth over a cedar

frame; we'll line it with soft fiberglass screening and make a door.

Three plastic cups, each holding a lump or two of old fruit, are lined up on the deck, surrounded by water. The first evening I'd made the mistake of putting them right on the ground, and by morning they were crawling with ants. So this time I put an inch or so of water into a plant trough, stuck in three upside-down flower pots, and put the plastic cups on top of that. Fruit flies found them immediately. Catching them will be something else again.

Pepys is ready for insects, and he already knows what he's supposed to do with them. This evening he saw a couple of specks on his box and he scrambled over to the side and stood looking up at them for a long time. Then he buzzed his wings and struck at them with his surprisingly long tongue.

I'm still taking him outside for flying lessons, but he's working up so much distance lately that I'm afraid outdoors will be dangerous from now on. If he should suddenly discover — in mid-flight, say — what flying is all about, and get away from me, he'd be in real trouble. He has no idea how to find food on his own yet.

With all the distance he's getting, he's still a glider. As soon as I take him out of his box, he arches and buzzes. He no longer jumps to take off; rather, he simply lifts off and sails, like a paper airplane, until he crash lands 30 or 40 feet down field. We're rather concerned — is there something developmentally wrong with him that he can't control his flight yet?

We're scheduled to go to a Labor Day party this weekend. We'll be gone three to four hours, and there's no way we can leave him alone that long. What if his syringe fell? What if the feeder turned around so he couldn't get to it? Pepys still doesn't know how to scrounge food for himself. He doesn't even know he can change feeding stations if one is empty. We'll have to take him with us.

Monday, Sept. 4
I snare a dozen or so fruit flies by slapping plastic wrap over the cup and securing it with a rubber band, and put the cup, nasty fruit and all, into Pepys' box. The flies leave, but soon settle back around the fruit. In an instant, the hummer's whole demeanor changes. He snaps his head back and forth, checking out the boxwood leaves, scrambling after any fly he sees. Good. I won't have to teach him what to do with them.

Flying lessons are conducted in my office now. I've secured two dhurrie rugs as sort of bumpers, and placed a few branches around for him to practice landing on. He's bursting with energy after having been in his box all night, and as soon as I lift him out on his twig, he's buzzing. He lifts off, glides into one of the rugs, and clings to it until I hold a twig next to him. He hops onto the twig. He can also fly, after a fashion, from one twig to another held six inches or so from him, and he knows how to land.

The flight cage is finished. Jonathan and I lug it up to my office after work. Since I'm at work eight to 10 hours a day, and I'm still concerned about what and how much he's eating, I want him with me all day.

When I return him to his Post Office box for the night, I put my face down near him again and breathe in his scent. He smells like a bird now — sort of cottony and green, like a clean aquarium, with a faint note, somewhere deep under there, of the scent of shellac.

Tuesday, Sept. 5
This morning starts off like all the rest. I go outside where his box is around 6:45, when he's just starting to stir, and offer him a little nectar. He takes it — but not much. I give him another 15 minutes and take him some Tonic-I/ glucose solution. He sucks it down greedily, and now he can manage the feeders on his own. Sooner or later, I figure, I'm going to have to let him get that first morning meal on his own. For now, though, I figure he needs all the help I can give him.

Later at work, as I lift him on his branch to transfer him into the flight cage, he buzzes and tries to lift off, as he frequently does when he's out of the box. Suddenly the light bulb comes on. He takes off, sails to the ceiling and buzzes all the way around, then tries to land on a picture frame and slides to the ground, where he squeaks five or six times. When I put my hand down for him, he does what he always does — hops onto my palm, using his chin for leverage, and settles down. I slip him into the big cage.

Wednesday-Thursday, Sept. 6-7
He's flying as though he's got a whole lifetime of lost time
to make up for, which of course he does. He has no trouble
landing now, and he can perch on a feeder. He's catching
bugs. How many, I don't know, but he's going after them
and catching them. He's turned into a hummingbird.

There are still a couple of big hurdles to go, before Pepys
can be released to fend for himself. The main one is
hovering. He still needs a perch in front of any feeder he's
to use — and nature isn't often that obliging. So he'll stay
with me in the flight cage in my office for the time being.
My Hillsborough mentor, Janine, says hummers can be
released any time that there's a guarantee of at least three
nights in a row above freezing. We'll work out the details.
For right now, Pepys needs another batch of fruit flies.

Friday, Sept. 8
I'm concerned that being transported in his Post Office
box with me to work each morning and then home at night
is unnecessarily stressful, so it's time for me to let go a
little, and for him to stay in the flight cage overnight. I'm
at work from 8 in the morning to around 6 in the evening
but he needs a little more "daylight" than that. I rig a small
lamp on a timer to go on at 6:45 a.m. and off at 7:45 p.m.;
that will give Pepys at least some illusion of "dawn" and
"dusk," I hope. It's the best I can do right now.

Of equal concern is Pepys' continuing mild morning
torpor. So far he's needed me to give him his first morning

meal; he hasn't been able to bestir himself to get his
engine going on his own — at least, not yet. Even though
tomorrow's Saturday, I'll be in the office by 7:00, 15
minutes after the small light has come on, to feed him.
He should be well awake by then.

So hard to leave him tonight. The flight cage isn't that big,
but Pepys is so little. As I'm leaving my office, I turn off
the main light and turn back to look at him in his cage.
The small light is on now, silhouetting him against the
back wall. He's on his favorite branch in his official night
position, almost vertical, his bill at 11 o'clock and his tail at
5 o'clock.

Saturday, Sept. 9
I don't make it in to the office until 7:15, and I hurry to the
cage. Pepys has broken his torpor by himself for the first
time. Maybe all he needed was more room. He's on the
fiberglass screening, squeaking and buzzing. As I watch he
zooms to the feeder perch and takes a long drink. Good.
One more hurdle down, and I can sleep in tomorrow!

Pepys needs flowers. He knows what feeders are for, but he
hasn't seen any flowers yet. Janine says hummers are hard-
wired for flowers, and don't need to learn to feed from
them, but I want him to have some. I spend the morning
tracking down any fall-blooming flowers I can find that
hummers might like: honeysuckle, pentas, butterfly bush,
hibiscus. I rig a little vase to swing from a hook near the top
of his flight cage and arrange the flowers in there. Pepys is

immediately interested, and when I hold the honeysuckle
up to him he buries his little head in each one. Then he
checks out the butterfly bush, investigating every purple
flower. I have to hold the flowers for him, though. I arrange
them so he can reach them from his perch.

As I open the cage to refresh the feeders for the day, Pepys
makes a beeline for the opening and before I can react he's
out of the cage and in the room. Zoom, up to the ceiling,
and zoom, around the perimeter once, twice, nearly three
times and he runs out of energy, just like that. Tries to light
on the molding, and flutters to the ground. He doesn't land
hard, but he sits on his tail, tiny feet in the air, for a good
15 seconds before he recovers himself, squeaks and jumps
onto the twig I offer him. Okay. I've got to set up the office
for him, places for him to perch. He needs more room to
practice flying anyway.

Sunday-Tuesday, Sept. 10-12
Pepys may be having a little trouble gauging distances,
or maybe it's the relative height of one branch compared
with another one. I watch him get ready to visit one of the
feeding syringes I've placed around his flight cage. He's
perched on a branch just above the target. He pushes off
the branch, buzzes in a circle, lights on the same branch he
just left and looks down at the syringe again, maybe trying
to figure out why he can't get to it. Okay, let's try this one
again. Push off, buzz in a circle, land on the branch and the
syringe is still one branch down. What's going on here? He
does this three or four times before he finally figures out

how to buzz down one level and lands on the right branch, with his reward in front of him.

He's meticulous about his bill. Each time he finishes drinking, from a feeder or from one of the syringes, he wipes his bill a couple of times on a twig. He grooms frequently as well. I give him a light misting each morning, and he fluffs and preens for 10 or 15 minutes at a time. His plumage is beautiful — except for his tail, which looks quite ragged, for some reason. And the little bald spot over his crop, which Janine says isn't unusual for them.

Meanwhile I've brought in some tall branches, with plenty of twigs of various diameters, and I'm placing them around the office, near the ceiling. Next time Pepys gets out, he'll have a place to light.

Wednesday, Sept. 13
I let Pepys out for his morning exercise while I'm getting his cage ready for the day. He follows his usual routine: up to the ceiling, zoom around the room a couple of times, and then he notices the branches. He approaches one, brakes, and changes his mind; buzzes around the ceiling again. He approaches, slows, shifts into perching mode and changes his mind again. Definitely, the little guy isn't confident with his perching ability. He tries again and snares a branch with his little feet. Okay. Maybe all he needs is a lot more practice.

Thursday-Friday, Sept. 14-15

Pepys needs more than I can give him, and he needs it soon.
More room, mostly. I've noticed a disturbing pattern of
behavior shaping up when Pepys is in his flight cage. He
likes the highest branch in the cage, right in front of the
feeder; he nearly always returns to that branch. But what
he's doing today seems uncomfortably like the mindless,
purposeless "cage behavior" you sometimes see with caged
animals at the zoo. I'm at my desk, preparing for my next
class, when I gradually become aware of his humming
buzz, every 15 or 20 seconds, and I look up at him. He's on
his favorite branch. While I watch he turns his head, dips
slightly toward his right, lifts a wing, and falls into a buzzing
flight in a tight circle and back to the branch. Over and over
and over, the identical pattern. Oh, Lord... I immediately
close my office door and open his cage; encourage him out
into the open.

Around and around and around the room until he's ready
to perch. He flies within four inches of the perch, gets
into position and slides down the air to the floor where
he waits for me to come over with a twig. He's not hurt
but something's wrong. Whether the tiny bird can't figure
out the mechanics of perching, or whether he simply ran
completely out of energy, he's not getting this flight thing
down as quickly as a hummingbird should. This, coupled
with the beginning of what may be cage behavior, leads me to
e-mail Janine: Should I bring him to you? She e-mails back
nearly immediately: Bring him on.

Saturday, Sept. 16

Pepys does not want to go into the small travel box we've
set up for him. He knows what the flight cage is like; this
little box is not his idea of fun at all. We've set it up with
branches, flowers, and two feeder syringes, and have
covered it with hardware cloth. Jonathan will drive us to
Hillsborough, so I can watch out for Pepys, make sure he's
eating (he still needs to eat every 15 minutes or so). The
trip takes a little over two hours.

Janine's sunroom is ideal. She's rehabilitating several
other birds, but no hummers right now. It's roomy, with
fiberglass screening on three sides, and undeveloped
woods all around her house. Pepys flies immediately over
to the screen and hangs there, wind ruffling his feathers a
little, sun slanting over him, just watching.

He flies around the sunroom and falls into the same pattern
he showed in my office — he misses the branch and slides
down the air to the ground. Janine points out that he's
bowing his tail unnaturally as he flies. I hadn't noticed
that, in my excitement that he was flying at all. She says he
may have been injured when he fell out of the nest. We'll
probably never know. But the tail bowing is keeping him
from lighting naturally, and impairing his ability to hover.
It also is probably what has caused Pepys to trash his tail
feathers, bowing his tail and pushing his bottom into the
screen whenever he lit there.

He may never learn to compensate sufficiently, in which
case Janine will probably keep him. Or maybe, with time
and enough room to exercise and build up his muscles,

he'll overcome this disability and she'll be able to release him – next spring if not this fall. For now, I'm confident little Pepys is in the best possible hands.

Sunday, Sept. 17
An early e-mail from Janine: Pepys has improved significantly just since yesterday. Maybe really all he needs is time.

Janine says that what I had taken for cage behavior was more likely his instinct kicking in: He should be migrating right now. His buzzing circles in the cage could have been his reaction to that wild imperative: Fly south now! Fly south now! Fly south now!

And surprise! He is probably a she! That black collar had fooled me. We'll know for sure on her next molt, when the throat feathers come in.

Even when we thought they were muskrats, we thought they were pretty cool. Muskrats on our little stretch of Briar Creek, which cuts through Myers Park. Muskrats, returning a little wildness to near-town suburbia, foraging at dusk and dawn, maybe even denning in the area.

They were indeed denning. But they weren't muskrats.

One evening in March, my husband and I were crossing the creek overpass when we paused, as we always do, to look for little vees in the water where the animals swam — all we had seen of them so far. Instead, on a sandbar upstream we saw five animals, including several juveniles. While we gaped the young ones lolloped in that unmistakable musteline way, poured themselves into the creek, raced in circles and slid back onto the sandbar to play some more, the shape and color of mink, but much larger.

They were *otters*. River otter, *Lontra canadensis lataxtina*, lover of swift, clean water — in muddy little Briar Creek? Voracious carnivore, needing a steady supply of fish and crustaceans — in *Briar Creek*?

Let me go back a few years. It was 1999 and I despaired as I watched heavy machinery truck-handling a delicate creek ecosystem for which, as a neighbor, I felt some small ownership. Workmen for Mecklenburg County Storm Water Services hauled large stones into the middle of the creek. They created a U-shaped barrier — a rock weir — across the water. They worked a mile and a half of creekside, piling riprap along the bank bottom, rolling out hundreds of yards of matting, grading the banks and moving large truckloads of dirt up and down the creek.

And they had the nerve to erect a sign that said
"streambank stabilization and habitat enhancement project."

Right, I thought. It may keep the banks from
eroding, but enhance the ecosystem? Not rippin' likely.

Little I knew.

Slowly, over months, baby sycamores and maples,
wild grape and jewelweed took over the banks, hiding
the riprap. So did mimosa and honeysuckle, unwelcome
exotics, but that's another story. Briar Creek's banks were
stable. As for habitat enhancement?

Within a year we saw the first Gulf Coast spiny soft-
shell turtle.

And then we saw redbreast sunfish, half a dozen or
more, quivering their bodies and fins to sweep away mud
and sand in the shallows, creating and guarding pebble-
lined nests. A Great Blue heron claimed the territory. A
pair of belted kingfishers chattered up and down the creek,
sighting for minnows.

And then we saw river otters.

"I think the return of otters to our county is
one important sign of our increasing sensitivity to the
importance of our water quality, and our success in
cleaning up our local rivers and streams," says Don Seriff,
conservation supervisor in the Mecklenburg County
Division of Natural Resources.

Seriff says otters originally lived in all areas of
North Carolina, but that they were heavily hunted after the
Europeans arrived. Worse than that was the degradation
of their riverine habitat during the 20th century. Otters
vanished. For decades they were absent from Mecklenburg
County and much of the rest of North Carolina.

But in the early 1990s the N.C. Wildlife Resources Commission began a program to re-establish them in western and Piedmont North Carolina. Why? "Most of the rivers had recovered by the '90s," furbearer biologist Perry Sumner says. He suggests that with otters gone, "there's a pretty major predator missing."

Sumner says they paid trappers to live-trap coastal otters, which were held for two weeks and fed copiously. "They're extremely adaptable, and intelligent enough to acclimate in a new place," he says. The Commission relocated otters to streams west of Marion. The plan was to locate them in Mountain Island Lake, but "when we arrived we discovered that they had already re-established themselves there."

This brings us back to that streambank stabilization project.

The "stone bundles" in Briar Creek created mild turbulence, and the weir allowed water to back up and deepen, the same way a beaver dam will. Both created new, varied habitats. Sediment fell out and the water became clearer.

"The hope was for habitat that would increase in macro-invertebrate counts, increase fish counts and add more dissolved oxygen to the stream," says Tim Trautman, one of the Mecklenburg County project managers. Trautman says they monitored the deeper, cooler water they had created and found improvements in all three areas.

And the increasing fish population attracted otters, which had not been translocated to creeks. "They came on their own," Sumner says. But they wouldn't have come without the cleaner water. Sumner says otters are a flagship species for water quality.

"It's great that our citizens have a chance to see these beautiful creatures swimming and playing in our lakes, ponds and creeks again," Don Seriff says.

But we cannot become complacent. Trautman says our streams are still threatened by pollutants such as sediment and lawn fertilizer, which clings to sediment.

"It's a tough world for wildlife ... especially those species dependent on clean water resources," Seriff says.

Trautman says the improvements to Briar Creek represent a cutting-edge environmental effort. Such projects are a challenge in cities, he says, burdened as they are with asphalt and concrete, and creeks that have been dredged and straightened over the years. Overall he is very pleased with the results.

"I was surprised, frankly, by how quickly some of the habitat came back," he says. "To see these results in an urban setting is really encouraging."

And to see river otters in the heart of Myers Park is just this side of magical.

Squirrels on the Seesaw

Cognitive dissonance, I tell my mass communication students, comes about when you try to hold two contradictory ideas at the same time, and believe them both. Your mind doesn't want to do it. Something's got to fall. But what I don't tell them is that every once in a while, if you hold your breath and don't squirm, you can ride that contradiction like children on a seesaw, perfectly level.

For a time.

I give you the squirrels.

First, some background. We live in squirrel heaven, a squirrel deli. We didn't know that, of course, when we began eight years ago to create a backyard woodland, full of wild native flowers and shrubs, so much more beautiful than those clumsy exotics. As for the squirrels — well, with just about every family on the block raising vegetables in the summer, and with the car the only large predator on the loose, the gray squirrel population has gone up and up — until this year, when moms and pops are wearing themselves out running spirals up the poplar trees and there's a baby squirrel poking its face out of every hollow.

The deli, of course, is the salad bar we've planted in the back: white and yellow trilliums with the scent of lemons; purple hepatica; bloodroot with flowers like little water lilies; masses of green-and-gold. Wild flame azalea, Carolina spice bush, Jack-in-the-pulpit. Squirrel magnets all.

While the little monsters leave the cultivated azaleas, the camellias and monkey grass alone, they dig at the base of every delicate, newly planted native, nibbling their roots and tubers, making off with the fragile shoots.

Year by year there are fewer trilliums; year by year our vocabulary of invective grows.

Inevitably, I suppose, given the population, a baby squirrel had to fall out of her nest. We warmed her, watched her open her eyes, introduced her to the world. Marveled at her velvet fur. Did you know a baby squirrel has a delicate scent, like clean laundry hung in the sun, only lighter, sweeter? She'll sleep under your hair if her nest is inconveniently far away. Her strong food preference is blueberries, at least until she grows up and develops a taste for trilliums. If you offer her a cracked pecan, she'll scoot with it under the newspaper, where she can eat it in confidence that none of the other squirrels that might be in the house will try to take it away from her.

Change of heart? Not really. I still break my heart over my struggling wildflower glen, replace the bloodroot and hepatica once again, mourn the tattered white trillium. I keep a stash of past-their-prime potatoes on the back deck to throw at any squirrel digging around the flame azalea.

But during a wild storm this spring, when a freak hailstorm flattened what was left of the garden, I sat on that seesaw at the kitchen window. I hoped all the squirrels were warm and dry in their nests, curled against a dozen siblings, their bellies full of wildflowers.

So, what's your prognosis, anyway?

It amazes me how good friends and caring relations, even acquaintances, who would never dream of asking me how much money I make or how much weight I've gained, think nothing of asking, casually:

"So, what kind of prognosis are they giving you, anyway?"

Do they know what they are asking?

Bottom line: I do have a chronic, serious illness. I do spend a lot of my time fighting it. I also spend a lot of my time writing, dancing, teaching at Queens University of Charlotte, researching about journalism, the media and ethics, tending my garden, playing with my niece and nephews, camping... I am not my diagnosis.

But still: "So, what's your prognosis, then?"

What do you mean by that? How long are they giving me to live? How long are they giving *you* to live? All of us, if we've been paying attention, have seen the "blink-of-an-eye" phenomenon in which, just because that bus turned left, or this young athlete ran an extra mile in the sun with a hidden heart defect, or the phone rang in the middle of the night, life suddenly changed forever.

Will I live to be 80? Or 70? Or 60? I don't know. Neither do you. Of course I look toward the future, and Libby's soccer game, and Todd's graduation, and Andy's newest art masterpiece. Of course I plan for a beach expedition, or a camping trip. I wonder if the wild orchids will come up next spring. But if I miss a single one of these "now" days, I'm the worst kind of fool.

Here's my prognosis: I'm alive now. Red-shouldered hawks are nesting down the road, and river otters live in our creek. Trilliums and mayapples are crowning in our yard. My husband is reading beside me, and a cat is asleep on my neck. I'm alive right now. This now. The only one we're guaranteed this side of the "Great Mystery." The only prognosis I want to talk about.

WORKS FOR CHILDREN

Josephine Jones had seven cats
Who wore fine collars and silk cravats.
And all the cats were Siamese
        But Abelard and Heloise.

Josephine Jones would brush their faces
And feed them in their special places.
And when she called them from their games
She called them by their regal names:

Come to supper, Scatmandu!
Sarsaparilla! Sweet Siru!
Sirikitty! Sniff-You-Please!
        and Abelard and Heloise!

Three things annoyed the Siamese:
Those awful baths. Those pesky fleas.
Those animal-shelter rescuees
        Named Abelard and Heloise.

Siamese cats are sleek and sly
With sweet-cream fur and teal-bright eye.
Siamese cats are swift and ghostly.
Siamese cats can do anything, mostly.

Siamese cats can tie their shoes,
Knot their mufflers, sing the blues.
But these Siamese liked best to tease
        Poor Abelard and Heloise.

Heloise had thick, silly fur
That stuck way out all over her.
And, far too large for a proper cat,
Abelard's ears would suit a bat!

Abelard had other woes —
Furry feet with six big toes
Enough to walk on snow with ease.
　　　　　(The same thing goes for Heloise.)

Siamese cats all know their names
And every Siamese owner claims
(As Josephine Jones found out real quick) —
Each Siamese knows one secret trick:

Scat knew how to cure fine leather.
Sassy could forecast stormy weather.
Sirikit rearranged the shelves.
Small Siru could conjure elves.

And Sniff-You-Please, both deft and sure
Won awards as a fine masseur.
No Siamese cat finds such feats hard.
　　　　　Just Heloise and Abelard.

When winter shadows stretch and creep
Siamese cats curl up to sleep.
They yawn and stretch and purr and dream
In a soft mound of sable and cream.

Which cats slept out in the yard?
        Heloise and Abelard.
And when the nights grew cold and damper
They slept in the basement laundry hamper.

One Christmas Eve (the house was still)
Siru woke up, as kittens will.
A clatter: Josie, home from the store
With a bag full of presents. She opened the door.

Siru found the Christmas bustle boring
And jumped right down to go exploring.
Nobody saw the shadowy cat
Slip out the front door — *just like that.*

The yard that night was deep and bright
With icy blue from the crisp moonlight.
And best of all, the prettiest sight,
A cottony blanket of gleaming white.
Siru climbed the cedar in sheer delight.

The kitten lost all thoughts of sleep
And took a joyous Siamese leap
Right in the middle of the pile of cotton
But what Siru had quite forgotten —

(Or maybe the little cat didn't know) —
Siamese cats *can't walk in snow!*
Their fur's too short and their legs too thin.
They break the crust and sink right in!

Little Siru, just nine weeks old,
Stuck outside in the bitter cold
on Christmas Eve, and *no one knew!*
She lifted her voice in a mournful *"Mew!"*

Then tried it louder: *"Meee! Meow!"*
She *had* to make them hear, somehow!
But the grownup cats were curled up tight,
And someone was playing *Silent Night*.

So wet and cold, she tried and tried
To cry so loud they'd hear inside.
And deep in the basement something stirred.
Something woke up. Something heard.

Which cats had ears like a bat?
And fur so thick and fluffy that
The bitter cold could never freeze?
Abelard and Heloise.

Those cats knew each hideaway,
Where every nook and cranny lay;
Those cats knew each place to hide,
And where to push to get outside!

Over the snow, as quick as that
Those snowshoe feet brought each warm cat.
Abelard dug beneath the cedar
And Heloise grabbed Siru and freed her.

And under the icy Christmas sky
They rubbed her face and licked her dry.
They settled her down, and each big cat
One on this side, one on that,
Warmed her with their fluff-soft fur.
Then — there it was — the tiniest purr.

All night they warmed her, nose to toes,
And while she slept, one bright star rose.
And no one saw it light the yard
    But Heloise and Abelard.

Next morning there were tears of joy
Hugs and cream and a new cat toy.
Miracle cats! somebody said
And two tired cats had a brand new bed.

For there in a pile were Scatmandu,
Sarsaparilla, sweet Siru,
Sirikitty, Sniff-You-Please,
    And Abelard.
    And Heloise.

Everything's Easy for Sara

Sara Felicity is in my grade.
It's hard to have lessons with Sara.

Here's what I mean: At Easter
Sara Felicity found *twenty-four* Easter eggs
and the stuffed bunny
and the spun sugar peep egg with the icing chicks
      and the sugar roses on top
and the plastic gold egg that you twist and open
      with the gold heart charm inside.
All the mothers gasped and gushed,
      and even our teacher, Mrs. McGonikle, cried,
           "How *ever* did you manage to find so many?"
And Sara replied,
      "It was easy!"
Everything's easy for Sara.

On Mondays, Sara Felicity and I go to music class
      after school.
We're learning to play piano.
But Sara doesn't play *Chopsticks.*
She doesn't play *Heart and Soul.*
She plays *Moonlight Sonata,* and at our recital
      all the mothers sighed and wiped their eyes.
And when Mrs. McGonikle beamed and inquired,
      "How *ever* did you learn to play such a hard song?
           Beethoven is very difficult, you know."
Sara said,
      "It was easy!"
Everything's easy for Sara.

On Wednesdays, Sara Felicity and I take Art Studies.
We're learning watercolors.
But Sara doesn't paint grass and tulips.
She doesn't paint clouds and sky.
She paints the jungle, with monkeys and parrots
and even a black panther,
      and when Mrs. McGonikle said,
          "Oh, my! How ever did you paint such a beautiful
          forest?"
Sara said,
      "It's a *rain* forest."
She was very clear about that.
Everything's easy for Sara.

Sara Felicity has a marble that is so blue
      it looks like my Siamese cat's eye.
It's so blue that when you look through it
      you can see the bottom of the ocean, or maybe heaven.
She won that marble from Jeremy Joseph,
      with her cat's-eye shooter.
Jeremy pouted and said,
      "I didn't know *girls* could shoot marbles."
Everything's easy for Sara.

From our school you can see my house.
I can walk to school.
And behind our school is a vacant lot
         that leads to the woods, and
         the woods go right down to the creek,
         and then there are more woods, and a path,
         and another vacant lot, and then you come
         to Sara's house.
I've walked over to see her lots of times.
But Sara Felicity has never, not once, come to my house.
I guess she doesn't want to be friends.

Sara Felicity is in my science class.
We're learning how plants and animals
         and people live together.
And tomorrow we're going on a field trip!
Mrs. McGonikle told us,
         "We can watch Monarch butterflies and swallowtails ...
         find pretty leaves ... pick seed pods
         to make dried arrangements for your mothers ...
         look for turtles in the creek ...
         We can even turn rocks over
         in case a frog or a salamander or even a *red eft*
         might be hiding there.
         Who knows what we might find."
Mrs. McGonikle teaches us cool stuff.
Jeremy Joseph didn't know that an *eft* is a baby
         newt. But that's okay. I didn't know that either.
"I can hardly wait for tomorrow," I said to Sara. "Can you?"
But Sara Felicity didn't say anything.

135

Sara Felicity wasn't in school today.
She wasn't there for Reading Hour.
She wasn't there for numbers or spelling.
She wasn't on the playground when Jeremy Joseph
       put his second-best agate into the marble ring.
She wasn't even in science class
     and she *knew* it was Field Trip Day.
Nobody would miss Field Trip Day!
"Is Sara sick today?" I asked.
Mrs. McGonikle said no. That's all she said.

When it was finally time we walked through the vacant lot.
     I was so excited I kept running ahead.
      "Look at the goldenrod!" Mrs. McGonikle said. "Over
         there, that's Queen Anne's lace. And just look
         at all the butterflies!"
We walked to the edge of the woods,
     where we could see the catbird's nest. There weren't
     any babies, of course, because it was fall, but we
     could see where the mother bird had woven
     yarn and feathers into the nest.
      I wish I knew how they do that.
We walked through the woods, where we turned over
     logs and creek rocks
     to see what was underneath.
      That was cool.
Mrs. McGonikle said the rocks in the creek
     were granite and quartz.

We walked all the way to the waterfall.
>A bullfrog went "plop!" into the water.
>A pretty turtle climbed up on a rock,
>>and stuck its head way up. It had yellow stripes
>>on its neck.
>"Oh, man, look at that slider!" Jeremy Joseph said.
>I didn't know he knew about sliders.
>A great big bird was eating minnows. I saw it stab
>>one with its bill. I found out it was called
>>a Great Blue Heron.

Beautiful creek rocks were everywhere
>One was shining like a treasure, so I picked it up.
>Mrs. McGonikle said it was milky quartz.

If Sara Felicity had been there, I'll bet
>she would have found a diamond

On my walk home I thought about Sara.
I thought and thought.
I thought so hard I almost walked right past my house.
And when I got home, I asked my mother
>to take me for a ride. When I explained why,
>she wasn't mad, even though she was busy.
We rode up the hill, around the curve,
over the creek, past the woods, until we came
to Sara's house.

"My mom let me stay home today," Sara said.

"But why?" I looked hard at her. "Today was
    Field Trip Day!"

Sarah Felicity didn't say anything for a long time.
    She just kept looking at the floor.
    I just kept looking at her.
    Finally she answered, in a little voice,
        not like Sara at all.
        "I'm afraid of the woods."

I stared at her.
    "You *painted* the woods," I said. "With a panther!"
    "It was a *rain forest,*" Sara said. "And I didn't
        paint snakes. Or a *red eft.*"

I almost said, "An eft is just a baby newt."

I almost said, "It's just the school woods. Nobody's afraid
    of *those* woods."

But I didn't.

I dug in my pocket until I touched my milky quartz.
It was cool and smooth as water.
      "I found this in the woods," I said."You can have it."
Sara rubbed and rubbed her thumb on the white stone.
      "It's beautiful," she said. "Did you find it ...
            deep in the woods?"
      "Just down by the creek," I said. "I can show you
            tomorrow."
Sara backed up a little bit. But she didn't
      give me back the quartz.
      "Did you see butterflies?" she finally asked. "I love
            butterflies."
      "Lots and lots," I said.
And then, just like that, I knew what to do.
I could hardly wait for tomorrow!

Before the morning bell even rang, I whispered my plan
      to Mrs. McGonikle.
      "That's a good idea," she said, smiling at me.
All day long I watched the clock.
Through Reading Hour
      and spelling
      and recess
      and numbers
      and lunch
      and The Colors of Fall Bulletin Board Project
      and tumbling
until *at last* the bell rang.

"Sara Felicity, would you like to see some butterflies?"
  Mrs. McGonikle asked, smiling. "I called your mother
  to make sure it's okay."
Sara's eyes got very big. "In the woods?"
"We don't have to go *into* the woods," I said. "We can
  go *just to the edge*, where there aren't even any trees,
  and there they are!"
I watched Sara's face. She was thinking.
Then she nodded.

She held tight to Mrs. McGonikle's hand all the way through
  the vacant lot, and then ...
      "Oh, look!" Sara cried. "Look at that!" She was so
      excited she forgot to hold hands and ran a few steps
      toward a bright orange-and-black butterfly.
Mrs. McGonikle said, "That's a monarch. And those are
  tiger swallowtails, and just look at that spicebush
  swallowtail! And do you see that butterfly in
  calico cat colors? It's called a *tortoiseshell.*"
Sara laughed and laughed.
Just then a tiny blue butterfly with little red dots on its
  wings landed on Sara's hand. Mrs. McGonikle spoke in a
  low voice, so she wouldn't scare it.
      "That's called a blue hairstreak."
Sara didn't move a muscle. But her smile got even bigger.

When it was time to leave, I got another great idea,
just like that.

"If you walk into the woods *just as far as that*
first big tree," I said, "you can see a bird's nest!"
Sara stood very still. Finally she whispered, "Really?"
"The birds are gone now, of course,
because it's fall," I explained. "But they
might be back in the spring. We could go find it
tomorrow after school, if you want to."
I saw another tiny smile beginning to show.
"You'll see," I said. "It'll be easy!"

I stood there with the flowers and the wind and the orange,
yellow, black, and cat-colored butterflies, full of
wonderful thoughts...

I can walk in the woods as far as the creek
without being scared.
I know where to find butterflies and birds' nests.
Mrs. McGonikle said, "Good idea!" to me.
I can make a new friend.
And it's easy!

141

Libby and the Hummingbird
Who Wouldn't Fly

Under the azalea bush at Aunt Jessye's house where ivy
grows lush and cool, and the branches make a tent
Libby loved to hide and watch the leaves and sometimes
cry because Vanessa was gone. Vanessa was Libby's
best friend, and now Vanessa's family had moved
back home, all the way to South America.

But what was that? Under the tent of azalea leaves
lay a bird so small that three of its kind
could have rested in Libby's tiny hand.
Libby parted the branches
and crouched so near that she could see
a sharp black eye, looking back at her
and a slender black bill, a third as long
as the rest of the bird.
And when the sun slipped through the leaves
and moved over the bird's feathers,
they gleamed more green than any leaf
Libby had ever seen. It did not try to fly away.
She laid an azalea leaf over the bird and ran for her aunt,
who knew all about taking care of birds.
She had a license.

"A baby hummingbird," Aunt Jessye said.
"She must have tried to fly before she was ready.
Or maybe she fell from her nest."
Libby and Jessye looked in all the trees, but saw no nest,
nor any parent hummingbirds looking for the little one.

"How do you know it's a girl?" Libby said.
"Well," Jessye said, "I'm not sure. But see how creamy
white the feathers are on her throat? I think she's a girl.
But whatever you are, little one, you need
something to eat, don't you?"

So while Jessye went to the store, Libby found
a box just the right size and filled it with soft cloths,
leaves, small branches and flowers.
"I'll call you Lacey," she whispered,
bending her head close to the bird,
but she didn't touch her. Lacey turned and watched
Libby's face through first one eye, then the other.

When Jessye came back she brought a bottle of nectar,
vitamins and protein, and a feeder just right
for a hummingbird's long tongue.
"Why does she need all that?" Libby asked.
"Hummingbirds eat flowers, and look at
all the flowers I've found for her!"
Jessye said, "Yes, she needs the nectar from flowers.
But she needs to eat insects too. This food will give her
what she must have to grow strong."
Then Jessye stooped so she was Libby's height,
and looked right into her eyes.
"But Libby, your little bird may have been out
of her nest too long. She may be too weak.
We might not be able to save her."

"But we can try," Libby said. "Lacey is strong.
I know she is." When Libby held the feeder
close to Lacey's bill, the little bird lapped and
sipped and lapped at the sweet liquid.
Finally, she fluffed all her feathers and sneezed.
Then Jessye held a small branch out toward Lacey.
"We shouldn't touch her if we can help it," she said.
Lacey hooked her chin over the branch
and pulled herself up, a little bird acrobat.

"She doesn't know how to use her wings," Libby said.
Her eyes were very big. "She'll learn," said Jessye,
slipping the branch with Lacey on it into the box.
"Now, we need to feed her every ten or fifteen minutes
for a few days, until she learns how to find food herself.
Do you think you and I can do that?"

Libby grinned. A hummingbird of her own,
to feed, to watch grow up and learn to fly!
"For a few days," Jessye said again.
"Oh, yes!" Libby said. "So we've saved her, right?"
Jessye didn't answer, exactly. "Let's go write Vanessa
a letter and tell her all about Lacey," she said.
But Libby looked down and shook her head.
South America was just too far.

"Now, don't go looking into the box every minute,
scaring Lacey." Jessye said. "Let her rest."
But Lacey didn't seem a bit scared. She hopped
around the garden in her box, climbing the branches
and pushing her bill into the feeder and squeaking
whenever Libby came over to Aunt Jessye's house.
But for days and days she didn't even try to use
her wings.

Until the day Libby noticed that Lacey had dribbled
food all over her fluffy white throat and green chest.
Now her feathers were matted.
"Lacey needs a bath," she declared.
So Jessye found a plant-spraying bottle
and filled it with lukewarm water.
Libby held Lacey's branch still while Jessye,
very gently, sprayed a small stream toward the bird.

And then – for the first time, Lacey reared up,
buzzed her wings, and flew straight at the spray.
"She loves it!" Libby cried.
Lacey played in the water until she was quite clean,
but quite wet. She quivered and fluffed
so fast that water flew like tiny jewels.
Now Libby had to dry her soaked little bird.
Carefully, she carried Lacey on her branch over to
the African violets, where Jessye had a warm grow-light.
As her aunt had told her to do, she held the bird
six inches under the light and very gently
brushed her feathers with Jessye's new makeup brush.
Lacey liked it. She turned her head to watch Libby,
fluffed herself, buzzed her wings, and settled down for
more brushing. Back in her box, Lacey preened her
feathers back the way she liked them.

Libby put her face right down to Lacey,
and blew lightly into her feathers.
"She smells like a fresh seashell," Libby chanted.
"She smells like my aquarium when I've just cleaned it.
"She smells like the sheets mom hangs outside.
"She smells like …"
"She smells just like a bird," Jessye said, smiling.
"Just like a bird is supposed to smell.
Now, stop sniffing her. You'll scare her."
But Lacey turned her head up to look at Libby,
and gently investigated each nostril with her bill.

Libby sang:

Lacey, my tiny bird,
You are so beautiful.
Fly … fly … fly!

And Jessye sang:

Honeysuckle, hollyhocks
Bee balm and four-o'clocks
Whole gardens full!
How will you migrate?
How can you build a spider web nest?
How will you find a friend or a mate?

"Aunt Jessye, what's *migrate*?" Libby asked.
Her aunt said, "When fall is in the air, birds like Lacey
need to fly far away, some place warm,
where flowers are blooming. All the way to
Mexico and Central America and South America."

Libby just shook her head.
"South America is too far," she whispered.
Jessye put her arm around Libby. "And yet a little bird
like Lacey can do it every year. Isn't it amazing?"
Libby stood very still, thinking. She didn't say a word.

If Lacey were going to migrate, clearly it was time for
flying lessons. Jessye and Libby took Lacey on her
branch to the sunroom, full of violets, orchids,
a ficus tree and golden pothos vines.
"It's a jungle for Lacey!" Libby cried.
She lifted the branch and the little bird reared way back,
buzzed, jumped off her branch ...
... and crash-landed across the room, squeaking.
Libby brought Lacey's branch, and the little bird
once again hooked her chin over it and clambered up.
All through the fall, Libby and Lacey practiced,
while swallows and monarch butterflies
and hummingbirds were flying south ...

All through the winter, when frost spiderwebbed
the windows and it was much too cold for a small bird
who didn't know how to use her wings ...

All through the early spring, when Jessye
brought arm loads of coral honeysuckle
and columbines into the house, Lacey practiced.
Each time she buzzed her wings as fast as she could,
but only sailed, like a paper airplane, until she'd tumble
beak-over-tailfeathers onto the Indian rug,
where she would sit, tail in the air,
until Libby came to pick her up.

And then came a bright late-summer morning,
the yard sparkling with hummingbirds.
A warm, sweet breeze blew in from the garden.
Lacey quivered on her branch and made her funny little
squeak-squeak call, looking all around.
Libby lifted her from her box, as she always
did, and took her to the sunroom.
Lacey reared back, buzzed her wings as usual,
and took off. But this time she zoomed to the ceiling,
whizzed around the room, hummed into the orchid,
and finally perched on the ficus tree.

Libby and Jessye cheered.
"She figured it out! She's a bird now!"
And then, all of a sudden ...
 "Well, would you look at that," Jessye said, laughing.
Libby didn't see anything.
"Look at Lacey's throat."
Libby looked and looked, and then ...
"There's a red feather!" she cried.
"One red feather," Jessye agreed.
"Lacey will have more of them soon.
You know what that means, don't you?"
"She's a boy!"
"He's a boy, all right! And I'd say it's almost time to
introduce our boy to the big outdoors."
Libby's eyes got big again. "What if he can't find food?"

"Just look at the flowers blooming now! And I'll put
feeders all over the yard. He'll be fine," Jessye said.
"And he can find other hummingbirds to fly south with."

They waited a week, until the weather was perfect,
bright blue, clear and warm. Lacey had practiced flying
every day, and was as confident as a bird can be.
Jessye and Libby brought Lacey in his box outside,
where they lifted the top. Lacey crouched in the leaves
for a minute, nothing but sky above.
Then he climbed up one of the branches.
Then he jumped to the edge of the box
and buzzed his wings...
And then he took off — *zip* into the garden, where he
immediately found cardinal flowers, *whirr*
to a feeder hung under the eaves and then *zoom*
through the yard to a tree next door and beyond ...
... and Libby's eyes filled with tears.
"He's gone," she said.

Libby and Jessye waited, watching the place
where he had been.

And then, Libby heard a hum and a little
squeak — and a tiny jewel of a bird flew up to her face,
brilliant green with one glinting ruby feather.
Libby stood perfectly still as the bird slowly circled her
head, squeaking into her ear, fanning her hair with his
wings. He flew back around to her face,
where he hung in the air for a long moment.
Then he was gone.

Libby's mouth was open and her eyes were wide.
"He's not gone," Jessye said. "You'll never forget him.
Besides, he'll probably stay close until it's time to fly
south for the winter. Maybe even in our garden!
And we'll look for him again next spring — Who knows?"

"Who knows?" Libby agreed. And she and Jessye
spread the flowers from Lacey's box all over the garden,
and walked back inside to write Vanessa,
and tell her all about it.

SPEECH

The Second Sex, the Third World, and the Fourth Estate

> *"The truth may be hazardous to those who tell it but is not dangerous; disinformation is. As I saw in Bosnia and Rwanda, it is propaganda that fans the flames of hatred."*
>
> *—Elizabeth Neuffer, 1998*

I'm a member of the Class of '74. Not college – I graduated a year or two before that – but a member of that class of women who stormed into broadcast journalism after the Federal Communications Commission ruled in 1970 that broadcasters had to diversify, to bring more women and minority reporters into the industry. There I was, among the vanguard, ready to "take on the world" and "make a difference." (You see, I already knew all the clichés!)

The time was the mid-'70s. The place was Raleigh

Now, politics in the mid-'70s in Raleigh was heavy with good-old-boy power: how rich you were, what color your skin, who your father was. Raleigh was led by legacy: middle-aged rich white men, following in the footsteps of their somewhat older rich white fathers, and so on and on.

Into that hotbed came Isabella Cannon. She was 73, she was tiny – four-feet-eight – she had a little bird voice, and she looked as if a stiff wind could blow her over. She was going to run for mayor.

Her opponents sneered: "Little old lady in tennis shoes!" Here's the way she answered: She got a pair of sneakers, slung them over her shoulder, and went door to door to door to door, winning over the voters, one by one. And she won. She beat the system.

Problem was, it was more than she had bargained for at first. Her meetings ran hours longer than those of her predecessor. At first she couldn't handle the complicated business and development issues that are part of the territory in a big city. And her opponents were quick to jump on her. The press, while generally writing objective stories, wrote about incidents that hinted at incompetence.

When it became my turn to interview her, I set up my equipment, we passed a few polite moments getting comfortable, and then I moved into my first question, something like this: "Mayor Cannon, there was a story in the *Raleigh News and Observer* this morning that ..." and before I could get the rest of the question out, Mayor Isabella Cannon broke down. She began to sob: No one was giving her a chance; this was all so hard; it was unfair; everybody was ganging up on her ...

And I had a decision to make. I made it. I turned off my tape recorder.

What I didn't realize until much later was the disservice I had done to myself as a journalist; to the public, who had the right to know what was going on in their government; and to Mayor Cannon herself. She wasn't young, she was under enormous stress – for all I knew she was in poor health – someone had needed to know.

To this day I'm not sure exactly what I should have done when Mayor Cannon broke down in front of me. But ignoring it was wrong.

There's a happy ending to Isabella Cannon's story. She got it together with a vengeance: She worked 16-hour days; she advocated for neighborhoods; she helped craft Raleigh's progressive growth plan. She set her own rules, and she won over the whole city. When she died two years ago at 97, hundreds attended her memorial – complete with bagpipes. Isabella had insisted on them.

I tell this embarrassing story on myself for two reasons:

First, to assure you that I did in fact grow up and get wiser – and, I hope, better at my craft. And second, to contrast myself with women I'm going to tell you about tonight. I was a woman entering journalism not just with my government's blessing, but with government's hand at my back, pushing me through the door; a woman in a country with a guaranteed free press; covering a story about government very badly. These other women work in countries without the press freedoms we enjoy here, certainly without government backing, and they are telling their story and getting it right.

What I want you to remember tonight is this: While grossly underrepresented in media all over the globe, women are pushing in, shouting to be heard, risking detention, risking death, and slowly changing the face of the media – the very definition of news – and in the process, the fate of women.

I've got a short overview on press freedom to start with, and then I want to talk about four issues: women at the margins of journalism, issues hidden by reason of of sex, a different perspective on war coverage, and new vehicles for women's voices. I'm planning to talk for about 30 minutes, and then I'll be happy to respond to any questions you might have. I may throw out a question or two to you. I can't help it; I'm a teacher!

First, there are some discouraging numbers on the matter of a free press in the developing world.

I want to go back to 2001 for one tragic loss:
Kuwait's first female journalist – Hudaya Sultan al-
Salem, the owner-editor of a political weekly. According
to Reporters Without Borders, a police officer admitted
murdering her because she had written an article about his
tribe and the traditional music played by that tribe. Hudaya
was one of 31 journalists killed that year.

In 2002 – 25 journalists were killed around the
world, and nearly 700 arrested. (This doesn't count the
hundreds attacked or threatened.) Nearly 400 media
outlets were censored.

And then last year – well, we've got some mixed
reports. By any of them, 2003 was a black year. Reporters
Without Borders reports 42 journalists killed – among
them, two women, whom I'll talk about later; more than
750 journalists arrested; more than 500 media outlets
censored.

Now, another research group, based in Brussels,
says 83 journalists were killed worldwide in 2003, one
third of them in Iraq. The statistics depend upon whom
you ask.

And as of this January, 124 journalists were in prison
around the world. In January, one reporter was killed in
Bangladesh, and two CNN employees were killed in an
ambush near Baghdad.

With tensions apparently increasing between
journalists and governments of developing nations, fueled
certainly by the conflict in Iraq, let's look at how the
second sex is faring as they begin to enter the Fourth Estate.

First: In many countries, women work, sometimes
in hiding, frequently in fear, at the margins of journalism.

Why? Several reasons. For one – in many countries, there simply aren't many female members of the Fourth Estate. According to the International Women's Media Foundation, the numbers of working female journalists range from a low of 2 percent in Bangladesh, to 6 percent in Nepal, 8 percent in Japan, 12 percent in India – up to a high of 35 percent in the United States and Western Europe.

But once again the numbers we get depend on who's doing the survey: In a study done by the Swedish human resource development agency SIDA, a Russian journalist reports that that 50 percent of her country's journalists are women. A Brazilian journalist reports the same thing – 50 percent. These reports are anecdotal.

And don't feel too smug about that 35 percent in the West: Indian journalists Ammu Joseph and Kalpana Sharma write in their book *Whose News? The Media and Women's Issues* that at least the media in India don't resort to overt sexism, racism and pornography, as do the "tabloids and the gutter press" of the West.

Second, as women make their way in a male-dominated field, frequently without government sanction, they risk their freedom, their health, their lives. Five quick examples:

- Canadian journalist Jane Kokan slipped undercover into Iran last year, scared to death because over the summer another Canadian female journalist, Zahra Kazemi, had been captured and tortured, and had died of a brain hemorrhage in an Iranian jail. And Zahra was in the country legitimately! Jane was undercover. But she passed as an archaeologist, talked to ordinary people and told their stories, and got out safely.

- In Kosovo, Aferdita Kelmendi saw her radio station destroyed, learned she was on a Serbian hit list – and finally fled the country with her family.
- In Ukraine, Tatyana Goryachova, editor of an independent newspaper there, covered stories on government corruption and malfeasance. She was harassed and threatened by the government, and in 2002 somebody threw sulfuric acid into her face.
- In Colombia, Jineth Lima covered the conflict between the government and paramilitary groups. In May 2000 she went to interview someone she thought was a paramilitary leader in a Colombian prison, but it was a trap. She was instead kidnapped at gunpoint, beaten and raped by suspected military gunmen.
- And in Nigeria, editor Christine Anyanwu was arrested and sentenced to life in prison because her independent Nigerian newsweekly had declined to endorse the government of that country's dictator, Sani Abacha. She served three years in prison, and was released after his death in 1998.

A sidebar to this story: In 2002 Christine received the International Press Freedom Award from the Committee to Protect Journalists, and as she was about to accept her award and speak glowingly of how much better conditions had become for journalists in her native Nigeria, word came down about a fatwa judgment against a female journalist because of a story she had written.

Remember the upheaval concerning the Miss World Pageant?

Journalist Isioma Daniel had written a story suggesting that Mohammed would have approved of the women in the pageant and might even have married one of them; and the judgment came down calling on Muslims to find Isioma and kill her. Christine said: there she was, ready to praise new press freedoms in her country. But after that, she said, she just couldn't do it. She took the award, said thank you, and sat down.

So women in many countries are working on the fringes of the mainstream media world. And to add to the difficulties they face, we move to the second major point:

Many human issues vital to women are hidden under the media's radar.

We do hear about the most atrocious news — the disturbing, the horrific, the noisy issues — rape, female genital mutilation, dowry death, sati (the system under which a widow is burned alive on the funeral pyre of her husband), sex determination tests and female infanticide. Those stories do make the news.

And why?

According to Ammu Joseph, who's working to promote gender justice in India, it's because vocal and active women's groups campaigned hard on them, and forced them into the public's consciousness. We speak of the media setting people's agendas, telling us what we need to be thinking about. Here, powerful women are setting the agenda for the media, who then tell us: We'd better pay attention.

Bear with me here: What is news, anyway? It's anything out of the ordinary. It has size — magnitude. It has consequence; it affects people. It has conflict. It's what people are talking about. It is what people in power are talking about. People make news, but not all people. The lives of the rich and powerful are more newsworthy than the lives of the poor and the marginalized.

Ammu and Kalpana write that violent atrocities against women are getting coverage in the Indian press. But what about what they term the "less gruesome but no less debilitating forms of oppression"? Issues related to women's work, their access to income, health, position in society and experiences within the family; issues commonplace and widely accepted – in other words, not out of the ordinary, and therefore not news. So the first issue that falls under the media radar:

The ordinary, extraordinary, exceptionally difficult everyday lives women lead, in lesser-developed, strife torn areas of the world. Tending family, sometimes in times of devastating illness. Holding the family together in times of conflict. Illiteracy. Tyranny. Routine deprivation.

From Africa, we get a big second issue, and that is health. In particular, poor coverage of illnesses such as TB, malaria, and especially HIV/AIDS. Journalist Colleen Morna says that while the daily violation of women's rights has finally registered on the media agenda – and on the political one – the link between gender violence and HIV and AIDS has not.

AllAfrica Global Media quotes The South African Police Service that 45 percent of men arrested for rape in the countries they studied are HIV-positive. Colleen Morna says that even if there are doubts about the accuracy of those statistics, "we know that the majority of those who rape fall within the age bracket that has the highest HIV-AIDS prevalence rate."

Even in the Middle East, where the infection rate is among the lowest in the world, Jordan's Queen Noor told a State Department writer that 55 percent of the victims are women. Noor says that 10 years ago women were at the fringes of the epidemic. Today she says they are at the epicenter. In the Middle East and throughout the world, AIDS is not just a public health crisis but also a women's rights issue.

And then there's the coverage of war. Strife marks many of the counties we refer to as lesser-developed or "third world." In my research I turned up so many incredible women's stories in this arena that I had enormous difficulty choosing just three to tell you about. I want to tell their stories because I am convinced of my third point:

Women have brought a different kind of perspective to the coverage of war.

Journalists participating in a recent survey conducted by the International Women's Media Foundation felt strongly that women bring a more human dimension to war news. A senior editor from the Philippines commented in that survey that men concentrate on quotes from government officials and focus on conflict and numbers of the dead, while women tend to look at the impact on the greatest number of people or sectors – frequently, civilians trying to hold their lives together.

An editor from Russia agrees. She says that women tend to show not only the number of people killed, but also the impact on civilians caught in the battlegrounds.

All the women whose war stories I want to briefly tell are winners of the prestigious Courage in Journalism Awards, given by the International Women's Media Foundation every year since its founding in 1990.

First, Elizabeth Neuffer, who wrote for the *Boston*

Globe, won in 1998 for her coverage of the conflicts in Bosnia and in Rwanda. (She writes about both in her wonderful, disturbing but ultimately hopeful 2001 book, *The Key to My Neighbor's House: Seeking Justice in Bosnia and Rwanda.*) Among her coups – interviews with the Tutsi women in Rwanda who testified before a war crimes tribunal in 1997. One of the witnesses was JJ, who told Elizabeth of systematic beatings and rapes, degrading, despicable treatment by the mayor of Taba, Jean-Paul Akayesu, and others. (The witnesses were identified only by their initials.)

JJ told Elizabeth, "I was wondering what type of death I was going to die." But she didn't die. She – and others – just faced rape, over and over and over again.

And then JJ said Akayesu made the statement to the other men waiting to rape JJ, the statement that stunned the tribunal, the statement I wrestled with before deciding to include it in this speech: He said, "Never again ask me if I know what a Tutsi woman tastes like."

The testimony of JJ and others finally got Akayesu convicted of genocide – the first ever conviction of the crime of genocide by an international tribunal. And Elizabeth Neuffer brought us the story. (She points out, by the way, that the term 'genocide' had not been coined when the Nazis were on trial at Nuremberg.)

A tragic postscript to Elizabeth Neuffer's profile: She was in Iraq last year covering the aftermath of the war, and she was killed in an automobile accident – the second female journalist killed in the Iraq war and its aftermath.

My second war correspondent is Anna Politkovskaya, who won the Courage Award in 2000 for her coverage of war in Chechnya. She has made more than 40 trips to what she calls "a living hell," refusing to be muzzled by the Russian government.

(The Russian government calls her "Russia's Least Wanted.")

In 2001, she was arrested in Chechnya and threatened with rape and execution. But she went again the following September, because she had promised a boy with severe burns that she would bring him money for an operation.

Then the night before she was supposed to receive her Courage award, she was called to help in the negotiations with Chechen rebels who were holding 1,000 Russians hostage in a Moscow theatre. In her talks with the Chechens and with the hostages she feared for her life. She urged the hostage-takers to let her bring water and juice to the hostages — or at least to the children — and she won that concession.

But food? No. "We've been starving," said the Chechen leader. "Let them starve, too."

As you may remember, before the negotiations could play out, the Russians stormed the theatre, used gas, and 67 hostages wound up dead. Anna Politkovskaya asks: "Did we do everything to avoid having victims? Is it a great victory, with 67 victims before anyone was taken to the hospital? Did anyone really need me with my juice and my attempts to help on the brink of a precipice? My answer is yes. But we didn't do everything we could."

I wasn't there, but I disagree. I read her account, translated from the Russian. She did all she could, at the time, on the brink of a precipice, with her juice and her attempts to help.

And many of you have heard Anne Garrels' reports

from the field on National Public Radio. She was one of only 16 non-embedded reporters covering the war in Iraq, and her reports earned for her the Courage Award for 2003.

Like the other women I've told you about tonight, Anne Garrels entered Iraq frightened for her life. When bombs fell on the hotel where she was staying, killing two journalists, she was just a couple of floors away. Still, it wasn't the bombs, she said. It was whether the Iraqis would take her hostage, maybe use her as part of a desperate negotiating strategy. She writes in her new book, *Naked in Baghdad,* that war dangers are basically the same whether a reporter is male or female. Still, she says she reveled in being a female reporter. "Men generally deal with me as a sexless professional," she writes, "while women open up in ways they would not with a man."

Anne Garrels reported every day, even when there wasn't anything new to report. "Sucking air," she called it. For her editor had told her that if she missed a day, her listeners would assume she had been killed.

What Anne Garrels did in her war coverage confirms what that earlier editor from Russia said about women being interested in the civilians, not just the number of casualties. She told journalist Robert Birnbaum last November:

"I just talked to people. And listened...Iraqis predicted very well what was going to happen. They predicted the confusion in the society, that it would split, and they described the fault lines and the looting that they anticipated. And that they were terrified of crime, and that there would be a security vacuum... They described everything."

The stories of courageous women journalists such as

Anne Garrels, Elizabeth Neuffer and Anna Politskovskaya lead me to my final point:

Though women remain marginalized, there are hopeful signs everywhere. Women are finding new ways to speak out.

One way is anonymously – for example, on weblogs.

Lady Sun is one of the first Iranian women to start a weblog – or a "blog," a blending of personal essays, guerilla journalism, photo galleries and support groups. Journalists have turned to weblogs in part because their nations maintain such a tight hold on the rest of the media. In Iran, for example, the Associated Press reports that the government has shut down 90 newspapers over the past five years.

A couple of entries from Lady Sun's blog:

Last month she wrote that she was afraid that after the parliamentary elections, the conservative members of Parliament would intensify their efforts to censor the Internet, and online journalists would lose their voice.

On the day of the elections, she wrote that two popular reformist newspapers in Iran had been shut down – for printing an opposition letter.

The day after the elections, she wrote: "Most of the elected people are chosen by less than 15 percent of the people's vote. Everybody knew the conservatives were going to win."

At this point she was writing just about every other day.

On Feb. 28, Lady Sun wrote, in a lengthy entry: *"People in Iran have never been silent. No fear has been able to shut them up for long. All through our history we have been fighting and getting killed for our freedom."*

And that's the last entry. The website is still up
— LadySun.net — but there haven't been any additions. I do
not know why.

In Iraq, the AP reports that young journalists are
embracing weblogs as well; they're protecting themselves
and keeping their sites active by using various nicknames,
multiple servers, and foreign-based blogs.

A sidebar, apropos of nothing: Another Middle
Eastern reporter is quoted in SIDA's wonderful 2001 book,
Women in Journalism: Female Journalists Making Their Way,
that if you go into any Internet café you'll find young people
at all the computers. What are they doing? Downloading
Western music.

Two other information-packed websites accessible
anywhere: AlJazeera-Net (aljazeera.net), the English-
language version of the Arabic station that took the world
by storm in the mid-'90s. It's also accessible in Arabic.

And Women's e-News (womensenews.org) is
accessible in both English and Arabic.

There are other hopeful signs:

For one thing, in 20 out of the 35 countries studied
in SIDA's Women in Journalism, women's groups have
organized to push women's rights and support female
journalists. In India, a reporter quoted in that book says
that women's issues are becoming mainstream. She
adds that as of 2001, women are occupying even senior
positions... in the forefront of the Fourth Estate. And then
last year a woman was named associate editor of *The Times
of India*, the nation's largest English language broadsheet.

From Africa — a group of men and women from nine
countries came together in Johannesburg last September

to find ways to challenge poor coverage of gender-related issues in the media. They launched the Gender and Media Commentary Service, to provide mainstream media with fresh perspectives on the news that affects women – and men.

In several African countries, female journalists started chapters last year to address the marginalization of women and women's issues. The delegations will train and sensitize all female journalists to defend their rights. A spokeswoman in Nigeria says the project so far has created "a distinctive African women's news agenda that enables independent news, written by women, to be accessed by women in communities using radio and other technologies, thereby bypassing the challenges of illiteracy and distribution."

Anne Garrels says, by the way, that radio has it all over television and newspapers when it comes to providing people coverage in underdeveloped countries. With little access to electricity, with high rates of illiteracy, citizens get their news from those little battery-powered radios.

As a critic for the *Chicago Sun-Times* put it, talking about Anne Garrels' reports: "A few choice words are worth a thousand pictures."

On matters of health – Amnesty International and Gender Links are working with non-governmental organizations across Africa to start a person-to-person and hospital-to-hospital campaign to raise awareness on the link between sex violence and AIDS – what to do after exposure, what drugs are available, how they are distributed and how they are administered.

Another quick health note: The Nigerian government

announced last month that Feb. 6 of each year – starting next year – will mark the International Day for Zero Tolerance for Female Genital Mutilation.

And in Saudi Arabia, a country with severe press restrictions, journalists who "dishonor God or the prophets by allusion, slander, sarcasm or denigration" go to prison. Reporters Without Borders tells us that there's an effort underway to replace those prison sentences with fines. Well, we take our bright spots where we can get them.

A delighted female journalist from Malawi, where democracy is a new experience, is finding journalism a new experience too. But she says, "I am like a child let loose in a candy shop ... It is very difficult to select the right thing... there are just too many sweets around."

For women in journalism, mark your calendars for May.

Two days ago, the International Women's Media Foundation closed the nomination process for the Courage in Journalism awards for 2004. Those names will be announced in May – one print, one broadcast, one health reporter.

Also coming up in May – Reporters without Borders will sponsor World Press Freedom Day on May 3. May 6, it's the IWMF International Women's Day.

And on May 9, the Boston Globe will award its first Elizabeth Neuffer prize, to support women journalists from around the world who share her passion for promoting social justice and human rights.

The second sex in the third world has made significant strides over the past few years as they enter the Fourth Estate. Despite being grossly underrepresented in most countries, despite overwhelming obstacles, women have found ways to make their voices heard:

- First, pushing away from the fringes to the center of journalism;
- Second, forcing media attention upon those issues that in the past have slipped under the radar, changing the very definition of news;
- Third, changing the way we look at war coverage;
- And fourth, finding new vehicles, new media to carry their messages.

As Elizabeth Neuffer commented when she received her Courage Award in 1998 — *"The truth may be hazardous to those who tell it, but truth is not dangerous; disinformation is... It is propaganda that fans the flames of hatred."*

I'd like to end by returning to JJ, the Tutsi woman Elizabeth Neuffer interviewed. JJ had to take a plane from Rwanda to Tanzania for the war crimes tribunal. Though she was terrified to fly, she did it, to help bring a war criminal to justice. But Elizabeth writes that JJ's young daughter, traveling with her, was enthralled. She was convinced that the airplane was going to fly her and her mother right through the stars.